CHOPPED

BIP WETHERELL

ISBN-10: 1492249041
ISBN-13: 978-1492249047

TO MY WIFE ELAINE...

Who has been there with me throughout the extreme ups and downs of our roller coaster life.

"Bip does for the world of helicopters what Dick Francis does for the world of horses." - Colin Dexter, *Inspector Morse*

ACKNOWLEDGMENTS

I would like to thank my son Steven for his invaluable input whilst writing Chopped.

I would also like to thank Rebecca Hill for her tireless efforts in editing this novel, and Graham White for his excellent cover art

THE FIRST ENCOUNTER

Michael McConnell was a teenager today. He didn't feel any different now that he was thirteen, trudging around his local estate doing his paper round. His Mum had promised he could have a few of his mates around the house on Friday night to listen to the new Rolling Stones album that she and Dad had reluctantly bought him for his birthday. At least then, after his Dad had gone to the pub and his Mum had gone to bingo, he could put the record on to his old Dansette record player and listen to it how it was meant to be played- at full volume. For now, though, things carried on pretty much as they always had.

Michael's paper round covered one of the council estates in Portadown, Northern Ireland, and, as always, he went and did his papers straight after school. He normally nicked a bar of Galaxy chocolate to keep him going till his tea but he hadn't had the chance that evening and, lambasted as he was with a constant drizzle of rain, he wasn't exactly in the birthday mood.

He put his anorak hood up over his bright red hair and walked briskly, huddled over his plastic shoulder bag in an effort to keep his cargo dry. He laughed to himself as he remembered a recent film he had seen at the pictures showing an American paperboy leisurely cycling down a street, throwing his papers in the general direction of the customer's front door. What a life! Here he was bending carefully over the always-too-small letterboxes trying to squeeze the papers through dry and undamaged. Mrs. Miles at number thirteen Pontins Street had chased him halfway up the road once for allegedly ripping her Daily Mirror. Michael was convinced it had been the scruffy little mongrel she called a pet.

The rain got heavier, so Michael took shelter in one of the enclosed alleyways that led to the back doors of the terraced houses he was delivering to. He stood a while, looking out at the rain lashing down from the iron-grey skies, overwhelming the drains and running down the concrete streets in rivulets. At the bottom of the road was the local police station. It had changed beyond all recognition since the troubles had started up again. Having once resembled something out of Dixon of Dock Green, with its quaint blue light shining the word 'Police' above the front doorway, it now had its windows and doorways totally blocked with anti-blast shields. The open courtyard where the police cars used to park was now full of army patrol vehicles and covered with anti-mortar bomb netting. But the one thing that Michael's Dad was always going on about and, to be honest, the one thing that got up everybody's nose, was the newly-installed flagpole. There, blowing in the wind, a huge Union Jack hung night and day, visible from all over the town.

Michael thought the flag would have been okay if

you were English or Welsh or something, but Michael was Irish, Catholic and poor, and was now old enough to realise that possibly the first two set of circumstances were the main reasons for the third.

It was then that Michael decided to bring an extra present to his birthday tea on Friday night.

*

Steve Allen wasn't aware that he shared a birthday that week with anyone locally, but he was thoroughly cheesed off about the way he was supposed to be celebrating his eighteenth. He'd only been a British soldier for four months, but here he was, doing his first tour of Northern Ireland, pulling night guard duty at the police and army barracks at Portadown.

When he had first been told where he was going to serve he'd had romantic notions about being in the same sort of American forts of the old west, where people would seek protection from the Indians. It was a hell of a shock on his first patrol when he discovered that the people he was supposed to be protecting were the bloody Indians. The only acknowledgment he got when he patrolled the streets was the odd stone lobbed in his direction, or when a younger and braver teenage girl would come up to him and spit in his face.

It had rained all that week every night, right on cue, as he started his shift at six. He couldn't wait until midnight, when he could have a few celebration beers in the dining room where a group of his off-duty mates had promised they'd wait up for him. He had thought about travelling a few miles up north to try out the nightclubs in Belfast, but had been advised against it.

Here he was, a British soldier in a part of the United Kingdom, and he was more or less confined to barracks. What a joke.

It was hard to stand there in the pouring rain, trying to keep a watch out for any potentially mortar-carrying lorries that might drive past, or scanning the rooftops for possible snipers, when all around him were rows of houses, their cosy lights shining from bedrooms and living-rooms, smoke rising into the night from coal fires. These small bastions of warmth and family were a welcome relief in an otherwise bleak night. It put him in mind of his own hometown of Corby, in the midlands of England. A town full of working-class steelworkers, with the same standard of living and the same mix of religion amongst the townsfolk, but obviously with less hatred of each other. The reasons or the blame depended on which side you were on, he supposed.

All of a sudden, Steve heard a sound that shouldn't have been there. It had come from the direction of the flagpole. He had long gotten used to the faint clanging of the wire retaining rope of the flag against the pole, but this sound had been different. It had sounded like a grunt. Steve marched over to the pole, rifle raised, blood pounding in his ears.

'Who goes there?' He demanded, peering up towards the top of the mast, squinting through the darkness and rain.

Too late Steve made out the shape of someone faltering, slipping then falling. A body crashed down onto him, knocking him to the ground and crushing the breath from his body. The figure scrambled away, feet slipping in the wet courtyard. Heavily winded, Steve struggled to his feet and gave chase, completely forgetting about the rifle that had been knocked out of his hands. He got to the fence just as the figure was crawling under a gap in the wire, and managed to grab hold of his leg. He started trying to pull the intruder back through, but overlooked the other leg, which kicked him full in the face. Steve fell back but recovered quickly, making one final lunge that succeeded in grabbing what he thought was the intruder's shirt.

'Leave it alone you English bastard!'

The strong Irish accent only made Steve pull harder until, with a massive ripping sound, the material he was clinging on to tore and he fell back into a sitting position with a thump. He could now see the figure. It was only a young lad, running away through the rain, waving something in the air above his head. Steve could just make out two things that would stay with him for the rest of his life; the trespasser's bright red hair, and two fingers held up at him from the boy's defiant left hand.

Steve looked down at what he had been left holding. It was half of the Union Jack.

Bloody hell, thought Steve, a strange sense of anger and admiration churning in his guts. The kid had been sitting on top of the flagpole waiting for the shift change just to steal the flag. If it hadn't started to rain as hard as it had, he most probably would've succeeded.

'Christ,' he muttered to himself. 'How am I going to explain this one to the sergeant?

THE FIRST ACCIDENT

Only seventeen and he could fly a helicopter. Scott Mason had always been crazy about flying. Even after witnessing that tearing explosion in the sky that had been the Space Shuttle Challenger in early '86, he hadn't changed his ultimate goal- to fly. He remembered the day well, walking home from his junior high school near Kissimmee, Orlando, his elder sister in tears at the news. Even then, on that emotional day, he had only been able to muster a strange sort of envy for the dead astronauts. Though it had been a tragedy, there had been a kind of glory to their end.

He had saved every dollar he had ever made towards his flying lessons. Nobody, but nobody, had pulled more hours at McDonald's than he had. So when he had finally passed his General Flight Test three weeks previously he had obviously been thrilled- but it wasn't until this morning, when he had received his official pilot's license from the Federal Aviation Authority and he had held it in his hands, that he had at last fully realised he was now a pilot.

His first phone call had been to his girlfriend, Cindy Lou, who agreed to meet him at Kissimmee Airport after school so Scott could hire a helicopter and show her the delights of Disney World from the air. He could now officially fly as pilot in command, with passengers on board.

*

Due south of Orlando, amongst the hundreds of lakes, was Florida's biggest- Lake Okeechobee. Renowned for its wildlife and excellent fishing, the lake attracted hoards of bird watchers and wildlife spotters in the late afternoons and early evenings. Mr. and Mrs. Marvin J Braddock were two such nature lovers. They had invested most of their life savings into their four berth twenty-two foot Winnebago camper van, complete with microwave oven, power shower, TV and video, all so that they could travel the state and enjoy their hobby throughout their retirement.

Today was another perfect day of Floridian weather. Marvin J had been fishing most of the morning, and Mrs. Braddock was now cooking his successful catch in the camper. He sat in a folding chair in the late day heat, his first cigar of the evening in one hand, a Sony camcorder in the other. He had been filming some nasty-looking alligators that were basking in the sun and snapping their jaws idly. The bulky camcorder had been a birthday present from his son, and was Marv's current new obsession. As such, pretty much anything that moved that day was filmed.

The distant sound of an aircraft engine caught his attention, and he busily scanned the sky, panning and zooming to see if he could locate the source. He didn't spot the helicopter until it had almost passed him. It was flying ridiculously close to the water's surface.

Marv focused the camera and started filming the daredevil pilot. He thought it was a nice touch when the young girl in the helicopter gave a friendly wave.

*

Cindy Lou waited outside the flight briefing office at Skyforce Helicopters at Kissimmee Airport for what seemed like an age before Scott appeared.

'Any problems?' she asked.

'No, not really,' replied Scott. 'Just a hold up on the insurance before they could complete the hiring agreement.' He smiled, the same excited grin that had spread across his face all day. Cindy Lou couldn't help but smile back.

They walked across the tarmac to where a fully fuelled Skyforce Two plus Two helicopter stood waiting. Cindy Lou had made a real effort to look nice for the flight, dressed in a printed summer dress that showed off her legs. Her long blonde hair was brushed to a fierce platinum in the bright sunshine. Scott noticed that the red high heels she wore might not be all that practical for helicopter flying…

Knowing that the Chief Flying Instructor would be watching, Scott took exaggerated care with the necessary pre-flight checks while Cindy Lou fastened herself into the passenger side safety belt.

Scott laughed to himself as he felt the pilot's license in the back pocket of his Levi's.

Cindy Lou smiled. 'What's so funny?'

Scott chuckled again as the rotor blades began to pick up speed. 'The CFI asked me if I wanted to do a thirty minute check ride with him before I took you up.

Can you believe that?'

Cindy Lou said nothing, merely shrugged. She knew less about helicopter flying than she did about pretty much anything else mechanical. She only knew that it made Scott happy- and, hey, how many other girls in high school had a boyfriend with a pilot's license?

The Chief Flying Instructor was indeed watching as Scott gently took off and bought the helicopter to a perfect five-foot hover above the ground. He was impressed, and had been careful to monitor Scott on his general flight test. He knew that Scott was a good handling pilot- all he had left to do was to learn to become a good airman.

Scott spoke into the radio. 'Kissimmee Tower, this is November Alpha Oscar Bravo Charlie.' He and Cindy Lou exchanged a smile at Scott's overly formal radio disc jockey voice.

'Bravo Charlie. This is Kissimmee reading you fives. Runway is in use 280, right hand circuit, you have no known conflict traffic and you are cleared to depart to the south.'

Scott expertly executed a 360 degree turn to visually confirm the air traffic controllers observations on no known traffic.

'Seat belt okay, Cindy?' he asked.

Cindy nodded.

Scott lifted the collective lever slightly to add more attack to the rotor blade, and by adding a touch more engine throttle he pushed the cyclic control forward to gain speed. The helicopter then entered transitional lift and commenced a five-hundred foot per minute vertical climb at sixty knots. Scott levelled the Skyforce at fifteen-hundred feet and headed due south. He deliberately flew away from Disney World and the Epcot Centre- he wanted that to be the culmination of what he hoped would be a perfect flight. If all went to plan, it would be just approaching evening when they circled round, and the Epcot centre would have just been lit up for the night.

'How do you know where you're going?' asked Cindy Lou.

Scott thought briefly of explaining that the Global Positioning Satellite computer on board gave his position down to two hundred feet. But he was quite proud of his map reading skills.

'Here, hold this,' he said, handing Cindy Lou the map. 'In Florida the best way to navigate is by the lakes. If you look on the map and find the airport, ten miles to the south you'll see a lake shaped like a horse's head.'

Cindy nodded as she found the lake on the map.

'Okay, now look down to your left at the lake below us, what shape is it?'

Cindy laughed. 'It's a horses head. This is real easy!'

Now it was Scott's turn to smile. Cindy Lou seemed as delighted with the flight as he had hoped.

'Can we go lower to spot some alligators?' she said.

Scott's grin broadened as he gently lowered the collective lever and started a gentle descent. This particular Skyforce was equipped with two radios, so he tuned the second box to his favourite rock station, where Bruce Springsteen was singing Born to Run. It wasn't long before Bravo Oscar was skimming over Lake Okeechobee, at zero feet and close on to a hundred miles an hour. Cindy gave a friendly wave to some tourists who were camping on the shore.

*

Thunder cracked in the sky like tearing sheet metal. Marvin J. Braddok was thankful he and his wife had packed up their Winnebago for the day as rain began to lash down and angry flashes of lightning began to disrupt the horizon. The famous Floridian weather had changed suddenly. It was the time of year that Mother Nature would get her own back after the days of hot weather by breaking into spectacular storms.

Marv wasn't scared of storms, but he was always wary of them. He still remembered vividly the time when he and his wife had returned from a holiday in London, onboard a Virgin Atlantic 747. They had been told to fasten their seat-belts one hundred miles from Miami airport as they had moved into an unexpected storm front. He remembered the violent flashes of lightning around the plane, lighting up the dark skies around them like the anti-aircraft fire in old war films. Most of all he remembered when the jumbo had dropped four thousand feet in a matter of seconds, throwing an air-hostess against the cabin ceiling like a rag doll and then, a few seconds later when the jet hit solid air, launching her back down to the floor like a missile. He remembered his wife being violently sick after hearing the twin snap of the air-hostess's legs being broken.

He wasn't scared of storms, but he'd learnt to respect them. You didn't forget that kind of unmitigated power in a hurry.

Marv paused and snapped his fingers as he

remembered something. 'Hang on, honey, I forgot the damn camera!' He quickly wrapped a wind-cheater around his shoulders and went out to retrieve the camcorder from where he had left it set up. He was just unscrewing it from the tripod when he once again heard the sound of an aircraft approaching.

*

Scott knew he was in deep shit. More and more he found himself looking at his instruments rather than outside. The visibility was worsening by the minute. An ironic smile passed his lips as he remembered his flippant remarks about navigating by the shape of the lakes. All he knew was that he was fifteen hundred feet above the biggest lake in the state going flat out at a hundred and twenty mph trying to leave this fucking thunderstorm behind them.

The air outside was practically black.

'Where are we?' Cried, Cindy Lou. She was peering through the helicopter's bubble, waiting anxiously for the next streak of lightning to light up the world around them. Then hopefully she could see if they were over solid ground yet or not. She was becoming increasingly frightened. Scott couldn't blame her.

'I think we're flying north.' He said, trying to sound as calm and in control as possible. This was only a gut feeling, the compass revolved around and around in response to the magnetic storm above them. The GPS only read 'Insufficient Satellite Coverage' over and over again. The next crack of lightning was simultaneous with several claps of thunder.

'I can see land! I can see land!' shouted Cindy Lou.

'Where?' Shouted Scott desperately, gritting his teeth as he tried to pilot the helicopter in the total darkness after the blinding flash.

'I saw the shoreline directly below us! I'm sure I did! I'm sure!' Cindy was crying now, desperate to be safe on the ground.

Scott gritted his teeth. He had to land the helicopter. Had to. It was then that he made his final, and fatal, mistake.

*

Marvin J watched through his video camera, using the zoom to search the sky for the approaching helicopter. For all the functions on the camera, it was hard to pick up much visually in the storm. The sky was as black as night, only to be lit up sensationally by the incredibly bright forks of lightning. At last he found and focused on the navigation light, flashing on and off against the dark backdrop of the storm. Now that he had found the light, he thought he could make out the silhouette of the chopper. Almost without thinking he pressed the record button with his thumb. As soon as he had done, the helicopter pitched upwards, its engine screaming as it started to plummet to the earth.

'Quick, quick!' Marv shouted to his wife against the roaring wind. 'Come and see! I think there's a helicopter trying to land!'

But as he filmed, the helicopter's speed of descent quickened rather than lessened. Then, as if he was watching a slow-motion replay, the rotor blades seemed to turn individually and, in a sudden flash of lightning, he saw the main blades drop and carry on turning till they chopped the tail boom of the helicopter clean away from the rest of the fuselage. Darkness returned, and Marvin could only hear the crump of the machine hitting the ground at over one hundred miles and hour. He threw his camera to the ground and ran towards the shoreline of the lake. All that waited there was a smashed and twisted pile of jumbled wreckage, silent and lifeless underneath the stormy sky.

*

Scott Mason was totally unaware he had a massive tail wind when he pulled the cyclic stick back in order to try and land. The sudden deceleration increased the speed of the rotor blades to such an extent that if Scott hadn't quickly dumped the collective lever, the rotor head would have spun away and joined the thunderstorm. But Scott had over corrected. The helicopter was now descending in its own vortex. There was no air to give the machine the life saving lift it so desperately needed. Scott's training told him he had to push the cyclic lever forward to fly out of the air pocket, but all he could see directly below him, illuminated by the lightning flashes, was the safety of the shoreline.

For the first time in his short life, Scott panicked totally. To try and stop the helicopter's descent speed, he lifted the collective higher. This only increased the angle of attack on the rotor blades, which correspondingly slowed their rotation speed. The low RPM light flashed on, the warning horn filled the cockpit with a screeching sound that was soon to mingle with the screams of Cindy Lou.

Scott's last physical act was to lift the quarter-inch steel bar that was the collective lever with such strength that he actually bent it in a final desperate effort to keep the helicopter in the sky. His last thought was a crystal clear memory of the spiralling explosion with which the Challenger Space Shuttle had decorated the Florida sky.

There was to be no glory for him.

A NEW JOB

The corridor of the Civil Aviation Authority's head offices at Gatwick, London, seemed to be a cross between his old grammar school and Bedford prison, where he had once spent fourteen very unhappy days after he was caught driving with over three times the legal amount of alcohol in his system. Steve Allen, Accident Investigation Bureau, CAA, smiled as he entered the restaurant area. The menu, dumplings and mash followed by cake and custard, brought the whole ambience of the building firmly down on the side of his old school.

Well, at least it's cheap, he thought, as he parted with a few pound coins.

He sat down and ate his lunch, tucking into the stodgy dinner and smiling to himself. He'd come a long way from the skinny seventeen-year-old stationed at Portadown. A short but eventful career in the SAS had added a firmer set to his jaw, a harder light to his eye and a thick set of muscle that even his years in CAA had yet to erode. Time and stress had pushed his hairline back to a pronounced widows peak, though his short ruffled hair was still thick and black, bar a shotgun smattering of grey at the temple.

As he ate, his mind wandered to his last visit to HQ

two weeks previously, when his boss, for the second time in his life, had offered him a sudden change in career.

The first time, several or so years previously, had largely been his own fault. He had spent six months successfully establishing himself as a deep undercover operative within the IRA when, at a highly publicised Sinn Fein funeral, his cover had been blown. He had been next to the coffin, standing stiffly to attention, when an English soldier had approached him.

'Steve, is it you?'

Steve hadn't been able to believe his eyes. It was his younger brother Chris, who he hadn't seen in three years. He didn't even know he had joined the army.

'Piss off, you stupid bugger,' Steve had hissed from the side of his mouth.

Chris had walked away, trying to act as if nothing had happened, and he might have got away with it if not for an opportunistic photo by a press photographer. The next day the funeral was in all the papers, with the same picture of balaclavas, guns firing in salute and, in the background, Steve clearly talking to an English soldier.

That night as he lay in bed he had heard the creak of heavy feet outside of his door. Acting on instinct, he dived from his bed and rolled across the floor just as the door was kicked down by two thugs in black jackets and balaclavas. He used the momentum of his roll to leap to his feet, bringing his arm around in a wide chop that connected perfectly with the neck of the first assailant, who dropped to the floor with a minimum of fuss. Not so easy was the second thug, who swung around an old Luger pistol and fired. Steve had managed to grab the man's arm, but the bullet had still grazed his shoulder.

Fighting back the sudden pain and nausea from the gun shot trauma, he had rammed his fist into the man's head as hard as he could, breaking two of his knuckles in the process. He then took the stunned man's Luger and shot him twice in the face. The thug's body had convulsed violently and then relaxed as the severe head wounds ended his life.

Sweating, breathing hard and nearly puking from the pain in his shoulder, Steve had knelt down to check the vitals of the first assailant. He removed the balaclava to reveal the long brown hair of a girl who couldn't have been older than seventeen. She stared up at him with lifeless eyes. Her neck had been broken.

Steve had been thoroughly pissed off.

It had taken him nine days to make it back to England safely, by which time he was feverish from his infected wound and exhausted beyond all use. Six months of undercover work had been rendered totally useless. The operation had been a total fuck up.

That was when he had been transferred from the SAS to the Accident Investigation Bureau of the CAA. That had been his first sudden and unexpected change in career.

For his first assignment wit the CAA he had been giving the sole directive of finding out who had planted the bomb that had created the horror of the Lockerbie disaster. He had spent five long years doing the world's biggest jigsaw puzzle, putting back together the Boeing that had been blown to pieces. He'd thought he'd done a great job working with the FBI and the Dumfries and Galloway police. He'd spent a further six months after that tracking down the bastards responsible for planting the bomb, and had been bitterly disappointed when he hadn't been allowed to take them down.

In the years afterwards he had been involved in countless accident investigations; a couple of mid-air collisions, a fatality in a formation flying team, even one or two micro-flight mishaps. And then, two weeks ago, his second change in career had come.

Niles Bailey was his CO, an officer of the old school, who, in his advancing years, was a man with more gut and moustache than anything else. He had been fairly informal when he'd asked Steve to take a seat, even offering him a drink from the brash and expensive cabinet he kept in the office. Steve had refused, having learned his lesson about daytime drinking the hard way.

'What do you know about helicopters?' He was asked.

His thoughts had gone back to his tour of Northern Ireland. 'Been in a few, sir. Mainly the Wessex Scout. It used to drop me behind enemy lines, so to speak.'

Niles remained silent, indicating that Steve should continue.

'I was an observer once in an army Gazelle. We hovered above cloud in the same spot for three hours waiting for a known terrorist to break cover from an IRA safe-house. Never happened. I was bored shitless.'

The CO finally got to the point. 'Commander, I'm taking you off accident investigation for a short time.'

'Why's that, sir?' Steve had asked, puzzled.

'Because, Commander Allen, I want you to do what might add up to be a little bit of accident prevention.'

'Accident prevention?'

'Yes. A Royal has decided to take lessons to fly a helicopter. It's a delicate situation. The boy's desperate to prove himself useful and independent. He seems to think flying a chopper will make a man of him. Lord knows why. Your new job will be to keep an eye on him, prevent him from being killed. Either by terrorists, or by screwing up and killing himself.'

Steve hadn't known what to say for a while. 'You're serious?' he'd said, eventually.

'Quite,' Said Niles.

'Bloody hell!'

Niles grinned under his thick moustache. 'Quite. The Prince of Wales has contacted me personally to explain that the lad is insisting that he learn to fly a Skyforce UK helicopter in Northamptonshire.'

'Why Northamptonshire?'

The CO had shrugged. 'It's what he requested. I suppose it makes sense from a security point of view. He'll be able to stay at his uncle's home at Althorpe Hall. Its only a short drive from the airfield.

This is all due to happen at the end of the month, Commander Allen, so there's a bit of pressure on. The specific machine he wishes to train on is the Skyforce Two plus Two. Needless to say, the Prince of Wales is decisively unhappy about this, and is only giving the go ahead if we investigate the complete Skyforce set-up; their instructors, other pilots, and so on. Take some time to research the company, and then come back and see me. I'll be sending you over to Northamptonshire for a personal inspection. I need a fully comprehensive report on Skyforce's suitability in two weeks.'

Steve had stood to attention, shook Bailey's hand

and marched briskly from the office.

Skyforce UK were the main distributors for the American made Two plus Two model, so Steve had begun his investigation by contacting the American parent company. He had received enthusiastic cooperation from Skyforce's Florida branch, who had realised the publicity benefits of having a royal fly one of their machines. They had sent over packages of useful information, company history, machine specs, even factory performance reviews. Steve had been impressed by the safety video he had been provided with, which showed the test pilots throwing the Two plus Two all over the sky; doing run on landings, engine failure recovery from hover, rear rotor blade failures. Twice helicopters had crashed but, incredibly, the test pilots had walked away virtually unscathed.

Interestingly enough, Skyforce had tacked on to the end of the DVD actual amateur footage of a helicopter crash in Florida. It was replayed in slow motion as the rotor blades chopped the tail boom clean in half. Steve could only sit there with a slight unease in his gut as the footage had switched to recordings by the fire and rescue service that had attended the crash site. The camera had zoomed into the crushed cockpit, revealing the broken face of the young pilot and the mangled remains of the passenger. Steve had figured out that the passenger must have been a young woman, but only because he saw the red high heel shoe on the end of a long, slender leg. The leg in question had been found several metres from the wreckage. The verbal report at the end of the footage had claimed the accident was entirely due to pilot error and no fault of Skyforce helicopters.

Steve had then pulled the personnel files on the people who would be involved in the training of the young prince. The managing director of Skyforce UK was one Martyn Shade.

He had taken the time to look carefully into the Shade family history, learning that old man Shade had built up a successful scrap metal business after World War II, becoming not only chairman of English Steel, but a celebrated businessman and millionaire on his own steam. When he had eventually received a knighthood, becoming Sir Henry Shade in 1983, the year before he died, he had earned enough respect and stature for the nation to be proud of him. Not so his three sons. Carl, the eldest, had remained with English Steel, and Henry Junior, the youngest, literally worked for him as an employee, despite the fact he was a shareholder and member of the board. Martyn, the second son, was not so willing to settle in the family business. He paid lip service to no one and, after leaving Oxford, did nothing except to represent his country at polo and shooting.

Martyn's blasé attitude to his position in life had changed swiftly on the day his father's will was read out. Carl was to be made Chairman of English Steel, the largest majority shareholder, as well as being gifted the family estate at Bilsdon house in Rutland. The rest was split equally between Martyn and Henry Junior. Martyn's reaction had been swift. Realising that he could never compete with his older brother in terms of wealth and power, he had decided to outdo him in the only personal passion they shared- flying.

Martyn Shade passed his general flight test to obtain his helicopter license only eighteen days after his first lesson. He was a superb pilot, but that was not enough. He bought some land at the local airfield at Bromsfield, practically next door to Helispech GB where his brother kept the company Augusta 109 helicopter.

He proceeded to build the biggest helicopter hangar in Europe to sell and service the new American 'family' chopper the Skyforce Two plus Two. Soon most of the UK helicopter owners were taking their machines to Skyforce to be serviced and Helispech next door was left with only one customer- Carl Shade and his company's Augusta 109.

One year ago, Alan Johnston, co-founder of Helispech GB, losing his business and facing personal bankruptcy, tied a rope to the hanger roof and tied the other end around his neck. He ended things swiftly and brutally as he accelerated away in his open top V12 Mercedes SL 600 sports car.

Martyn had been characteristically callous to his rivals suicide, even going as far as to employ one of Alan's twin daughters, Valerie, as his secretary. Speculation in the intelligence suggested the two were having an affair behind the back of Martyn's wife.

Steve had smiled grimly to himself as he read over the extensive notes he had made on the Shade family. It all read like a script for a daytime soap opera. He didn't think he'd ever understand the cutthroat world of the super rich, but it was clear Martyn had certainly done well for himself; making enormous profit from his helicopter sales business he now had the capital to back his playboy lifestyle. Having a royal learning to fly in a Skyforce machine would certainly be a feather in his cap, Steve reflected.

As well as his research on the Skyforce company, Steve had also taken an interest in the type of person they catered for. As he had browsed through the membership roster of the All-England Helicopter Club he noted that, as well as famous television presenters and radio personalities, there was even an MP who flew his own Skyforce helicopter- one Rupert Cooksely, a former farmer from Northamptonshire.

It had been a busy week, turning up a lot of drama and information that was certainly interesting. However, from a security perspective, the whole set up was reassuringly bland. There didn't seem to be any skeletons in the closet that would suggest that Skyforce was anything less than a professional and reputable company. If that was the case, then his personal inspection would be a walk in the park.

Steve finished his lunch, leaving half of the cake and custard uneaten. He walked back to Bailey's office, ready to give him what he felt was a totally comprehensive preliminary report into the Skyforce set up.

THE HI-JACK

Rupert Cooksley was fifty-nine years old, but spent a lot of time and money concealing that particular fact. With the swept back and expertly coloured hair, coupled with the South-of-France tan and the gym-conditioned body, he could easily pass for forty or so- an essential deception when he frequented the gay bars of London. And frequent them he did, using his natural charm and bulging wallet to ensnare men under half his age. Not that he could ever be seen leaving with them. Rupert Cooksley, other than being a well-to-do farmer from Northamptonshire, was also an MP of high standing and reputation. His sexual preference for men was something he went to great lengths to conceal.

In the public eye he was the consummate family man; indeed, family values was always at the spearhead of his political approach. In private, however, his fourteen-year-old son rarely spoke to him, and his relationship with his wife was strictly professional. She no longer shared his bed, but still willingly shared his money. Until recently Marie had even provided Rupert's rent-boys, driving down to Soho to buy his sex for the weekend. The arrangement had worked perfectly well for a number of years- the police hardly likely to arrest a middle-aged woman as a kerb-crawler- but it had all come to an abrupt end after a phone-call from the Daily Card. The newspapers three-month long Slam Down on Sleaze campaign had thrown a lot of the after-hours activities of politicians into the spotlight, and Rupert Cooksley had nearly become a victim of the media witch-hunt. It had cost him £100,000 to bury the publication, and illicit trips to Soho became a luxury he could no longer afford. He had had to think of something else…

The answer came in the shape of a Skyforce Two plus Two helicopter. Three months of solid training at Skyforce UK meant that he could commute from the purpose-built hanger in the paddock behind his house to the Battersea Heliport, London. It was the ultimate in discreet private transport, and suited his needs perfectly.

Cooksley reflected on his changing fortunes as he went through his pre-flight checklist, waiting as the sun set over Battersea. Today had been a good day. An early departure from home had meant that only an hour later he was following the River Thames into London. As always the view had been incredible, and Rupert had wondered if he'd one day have the nerve to fly under Tower Bridge. Flying had become something of a passion for him, much more than the original means-to-an-end he had intended it to be.

That day he had given a rousing, televised speech in parliament in the House of Commons, begging more money for the redundant steelworkers in his constituency. It had been a great speech, honest and earthy and very blue collar. It would mean fuck all in the long run as far as the steelworkers were concerned, but it had been great for his image.

He had nearly been made late for his lunch appointment at Diva's by some sort of security kerfuffle at the House. Apparently some washed-up terrorist was to walk free from Pentonville prison that day- let-off early through some pork-barrel politic negotiations- and a few of the higher-ups thought that he might still bear enough of a grudge against English politics and politicians to pose a security threat. Rupert had managed to keep the lunch appointment though, and had made some delicate negotiations concerning his departure from London, and who would be departing with him…

He had completed all the checks his helicopter required, paid his landing fee and had 'booked out' with the control tower. Now all he had to do was wait on his passenger. He checked his watch. The pre-arranged taxi arrived almost exactly on time. A nineteen-year old vision emerged from the rear door, delightfully skinny, with a girlish lilt to his hips. His jet-black hair was carefully ruffled into a fashionable mess and razor sharp cheekbones framed his pouty lips. Rupert couldn't keep the smile from his face as his weekend companion got into the passenger side, put on his headphones and closed the doors. Rupert didn't say a word, just started the engine, monitored the rotor blade revs and, whilst waiting for the cylinder heads to warm to their operating temperature, called Battersea radio for permission to depart.

It was just after Battersea had given Golf Oscar Charlie Zulu Bravo clearance that the planned weekend of passion for Rupert Cooksley MP came to an abrupt and horrifying end.

When Rupert first felt the prod of metal in the back of his neck he had thought it was his young, soon-to-be lover, pissing about. Due to noise of the engine and his concentration on what he was doing, he hadn't heard the back door open. He turned around sharply, only for irritation to turn to shock as he stared into the twin black holes of a sawn-off shotgun. His first impression was that he had somehow upset his rent-boy's pimp, but a quick glance to his left confirmed that he wasn't the only one who was shit-scared.

The uninvited passenger climbed into the restricted space behind the pilot and motioned for Rupert to take off. Climbing away from the heliport wasn't easy at the best of times- the wind never seemed to be in the right direction, and accurate flying was imperative to ensure a pilot didn't infringe on Heathrow's airspace. Rupert nearly lost control as his left hand froze on the collective lever while his right hand shook madly on the cyclic control. His concentration was distilled greatly, however, when he felt the sharp press of a firearm in the back of his head. He managed to level the chopper off at one thousand feet.

'Dublin.'

Rupert barely heard the command over the noise of the rotor blades, so distracted was he in keeping the helicopter flying straight. He went to turn around, and received a sharp blow to the head for his troubles. Not enough to jar him, but certainly enough to get the point across.

'Dublin,' the intruder repeated, revealing a strong Irish accent.

Rupert opened his mouth to reply that the idea was preposterous- that reaching Dublin would be a long shot at best. He thought better of it, though, clearly remembering the feel of that solid steel on the back of his cranium. Instead he silently thanked God that the mechanics had refuelled both of his tanks that day for his return trip. With any luck, fuel endurance wouldn't be a problem in getting to Southern Ireland.

Suddenly it dawned on Rupert- could this be the ex-terrorist that went free from Pentonville earlier today? But why would he be hijacking a helicopter if he was a free man? Rupert wished he'd paid more attention back at the House rather than fussing about his lunch appointment at Diva's.

Playing it safe, Rupert switched off his radio and decided to fly low level, keeping clear of Manchester and Birmingham airspace. He set his GPS computer to a direct route to Dublin. His hands briefly hovered above his transponder- he had the option to key in the international four-digit code for Terrorist On Board, but his courage failed him. He switched it off, vying to play things as safe as possible, hoping that in an hour or so he could land, get rid of his unwanted passenger, and get home.

He flew on through the evening for what seemed like an age, his teeth clenched and his palms sweating as the Irishman behind him sat in total silence.

A voice came through the headsets. 'Please.'

Rupert winced. Part of him wanted to tell the rent-boy to shut his mouth, just to sit there and be quiet and everything would be fine. Fear held his tongue in his mouth.

'Please.' Said the young lad, his voice quiet and level on the radio. Not quite pleading, almost negotiating, appealing. Tears were running down his face in a steady stream. He had yet to break down and sob, but a dark stain in his crotch gave away just how terrified he was.

'Please. Please.'

The Irishman didn't even look at him. He swung the sawn-off shotgun in the direction of the young man's face and pulled the trigger for a single barrel shot. The boy had time to raise a hand to protect his face. A futile gesture. There was an almighty boom and his fingers were blown off, shredded by the same shot that then hollowed out most of his face. His body went limp, blood squirting from where his jaw used to be like some house-of-horrors cadaver.

Rupert looked on in frozen horror as the intruder calmly reached over and unclasped the safety belt around the corpse, and then, with no ceremony, opened the passenger door for it to fall out into the Irish Sea. He felt nausea threatening to overwhelm him, and for a moment was sure he was trapped in some maddening fever dream.

The Irishman shut the door, struggled into the front of the chopper, put on the headset and stretched his legs out, as though coming home from a long day at work. Rupert hadn't realised how tall the intruder was, or how thick and ropey he was with muscle. It was hard to see much of his face beneath a black woollen hat and thick black moustache and beard, but Rupert guessed that the man must have been approaching his forties. It quickly occurred to Rupert that paying so much attention to the appearance of the violent killer in his helicopter might not be such a great idea. He choked back a sob. Suddenly, he knew beyond a shadow of a doubt that he was going to die.

He didn't, though. They just flew on, eventually coming in over Irish lands.

Rupert finally worked up the nerve to speak. 'I'll have to land you on the beach, otherwise we'll be spotted.'

The big man only nodded his approval.

Cooksley nearly lost the helicopter as he landed on the first available piece of coastline. Firstly, one of the skids had started to sink into the sand, and secondly Rupert was fully expecting to have his head blown off at any moment, which made his movements shaky and unreliable. But the big Irish lad had simply got out of the helicopter, turned, said 'I'll be in touch' and then walked away.

Rupert had leaned over, shut the door and took off like a cork coming out of a bottle. Straight up and back to England, refuelling at the first available opportunity.

A few hours later he was sitting next to the log fire in his living room, still shaking despite the heat and the half-empty tumbler of brandy in his hand. It had taken him the best part of an hour to clean the passenger seat of the Two plus Two. He remembered with a shudder picking out tiny pieces of skull from the creases in the seats. The heady stench of blood and disinfectant was still thick in his nose.

He nearly jumped out of his skin when the phone rang. He picked up the receiver, wondering briefly what else could possibly surprise him today.

'Hello, Rupert Cooksley MP.' The deep accented voice was all too familiar. After all, he had heard it spoken not two hours ago.

'Owner of helicopter Golf Oscar Charlie Zulu Bravo. Not a word about me, boyo, not if you don't want the world to know about your pretty young boyfriends. Not a fucking word.'

The line went dead. Rupert stood there with the receiver in his hand for a long time, the phone beeping its disapproval. He couldn't believe what had happened. He, an English MP, had just aided and abetted a vicious criminal, and no one, but no one, knew about it.

Well, someone had, but his pretty young face was broken and torn at the bottom of the Irish Sea.

THE FIRST INCIDENT

Steve Allen was making good progress driving north up the A1. He wasn't the most stylishly dressed of men by any stretch of the word, and the decoration in his boxy flat in London was sparse at best, but he really took pride in his car. The black Lexus two-door coupe was polished to a gleam as it sped along the motorway, purring steadily at two and half thousand revs, the speedometer never wavering from the hundred mile an hour mark. A custom sound system boomed a euphoric rock ballad, complementing the unseasonable sunshine of the day and Steve's good mood in general.

The volume adjusted suddenly as his car phone came through the speakers automatically.

'Hi, Steve Allen here.'

'Hello, Mr. Allen, this is Valerie Johnson, secretary to Martyn Shade.'

Steve thought back to the detailed file he had built up on the Johnson twins. *More than just a secretary*, he thought.

'What can I do for you?' He said.

'Just a quick call to say I've managed to book you a room at Rambleton Hall near Oakham for the next couple of days. I'm sure you'll like it, and it's fairly close to the airfield.'

'Very kind,' Steve said. He would have been perfectly satisfied with a Travel Lodge, but if Skyforce where insisting on footing the bill for one of England's finest hotels, he wasn't going to argue.

'Another thing, Mr. Shade might be a little late for your nine o' clock. We're currently running a European Safety course for Skyforce customers and Martyn likes to handle the introductions himself before handing over to our CFI. If you like I could give you the guided tour while you're waiting?'

'Sounds great,' said Steve. 'I'll see you at nine.'

Steve hung up the phone and keyed in the address for Rambleton Hall into his Sat-Nav. He turned his music back up to hear Bono shouting it's a beautiful day, over the background of the feel good power chords synonymous with U2. He smiled to himself. He had to agree, it certainly was turning out nice.

The first indication that he was approaching his destination was the postcard panorama of Rutland Water. Steve had read up enough on the history of the area to know that Rutland Water was a manmade lake, though the church spire that erupted crookedly from the centre was clue enough to that. The nature of his career meant that Steve had spent a lot of his time travelling around Britain, but some of the understated gems of English countryside still left him impressed. It was all a far cry from the grey streets of London.

He spotted the turn off for Rambleton Hall and turned on to a long road that eventually turned to an equally long gravel drive. He pulled up at the impressive looking old building, resplendent with gothic style architecture, restored and maintained with obvious care and attention. A valet was waiting at the door to take his car while a uniformed porter showed him directly to his room. Steve was pleased. His more than spacious room opened onto stunning views of the lake, and as he sat down on the perfectly made bed he reflected that, if this was the high life, then he could definitely get used to it.

He briefly contemplated a visit to the bar, but he knew that one drink would lead to another, and he had a busy day to follow. Instead he unpacked his meagre suitcase, sat down on the astonishingly comfortable bed and settled in for an early night.

The following morning he rose earlier than he needed to, taking the opportunity for a jog around the grounds as the sun was just rising in the sky. After a shower he set off to Bromsfield Aerodrome and arrived with plenty of time to spare before his nine o' clock. He used the time to take a drive around the perimeter, stopping at a beautifully tended war memorial listing the names of the American airmen who had lost their lives over Germany whilst carrying out bombing raids in the 'Flying Fortresses'. Steve could see that one of the runways had long since been ploughed over, but another was still in use, accommodating a flying school that managed to run a couple of Cessna 150's from it.

He shifted his attention to the old World War II hangers that hung huge and stolid on the flat landscape. He could see one with a sign above it that said Helispech GB. He smiled grimly as he remembered his research on the failing company, and wondering if this was the hangar where Alan Johnston had decapitated him self. His gaze travelled past an old air traffic control tower (another relic from the war) and onto the Skyforce HQ. Far different from the seemingly abandoned Helispech GB hangar, Skyforce presented a front expected of a flourishing business. Twin car parks at the front, one for staff and one sign-posted for visitors, lead on to the complete glass frontage of the executive offices. A large purpose-built hangar sat just behind. The hangar was big, but apparently not big enough, as Steve counted at least a dozen Skyforce Two plus Twos lined up outside next to the fuelling pumps. He got back into his Lexus and drove around the perimeter road and into the Skyforce HQ visitor parking area.

He walked through the automatic sliding doors, immediately feeling inappropriately dressed in his Levi's and leather jacket. The general ambience of the building seemed to demand an Armani suit and a Rolex watch. He declined the receptionist's offer of a coffee and took a seat.

Almost as soon as he had sat down he stood up again as a woman entered the room. She was the type that was clearly used to commanding attention; everything about the way she carried herself seemed to hint at sex and power. A tight fitting suit and skirt combination was at the same time professional and alluring, her ice-white hair cascaded like a platinum waterfall onto her shoulders. Her lips were movie-star red, her skin expensively tanned to perfection. All of these features, however, took a back seat to her eyes, which were a deep-down blue and as piercing as a bullet from a gun. She fixed him with a gaze that- casual as it was- seemed to hint at a probing intimacy.

'Steve Allen?' she said.

Steve nodded, temporarily lost for words.

'I'm Val, we spoke on the phone.'

'Of course,' said Steve. 'Nice to meet you.'

They shook hands, Steve wondering how a handshake could be both delicate and firm at the same time. He caught himself guessing how old she was; she carried herself with the comfortable confidence of a woman approaching middle-age, but her figure and looks were so pristine she could easily pass for mid-twenties.

Steve realised he was staring...

'I'm not late am I?' he said, quickly.

'Not at all. Come with me and I'll take you through to the training school.'

Valerie Johnson made all the usual small talk as they walked- was his trip okay, was the hotel as nice as she had heard- and Steve made all the right noises while trying to drag his attention away from the swaying hips in front of him so that he could concentrate on where he was walking.

Val put a finger to her lips to indicate they should be quiet, and then led him through to a large lecture room where more than a dozen people were sitting, listening attentively to the man in front of them. Steve recognised Martyn Shade from the photos in his file, but they couldn't have hinted at the sheer scale of the man. He stood at least six-foot and four inches, and his shoulders were broadened from hours of gym work. He wore a tailor cut suit that probably cost more than a month of Steve's salary. He was impressive, suiting his thirty-three years well, a head of dark blonde hair curled delicately at the sides and back in a style more suited to a surf-bum than a corporate exec. When he spoke, he spoke with the rich tones of the entirely confident, a confidence born of total self-belief.

'Good morning, everyone,' he boomed. 'Welcome to the European Safety course. It is the purpose of the next few days to improve the skills, attitude and awareness of private helicopter pilots, through a series of practical courses, engineering demonstrations and new European Safety legislation orientation. Rest assured, the word you will be hearing again and again for the duration of this course is safety. After all, a good pilot is a safe pilot...'

As Martyn carried on with his introduction Steve took the opportunity to observe the audience. He recognised two radio disc jockeys immediately, and smiled as he recalled the recent effort by one of them to become a racing driver, hoping that the DJ would have more luck with his flying than the he did with the formula 3000 car he had smashed into a wall at nearby Silverstone. Steve carried on scanning the crowds, two female pilots standing out in the mostly male audience. Then he saw a face that he recognised from his case file- that of the local MP, Rupert Cooksley.

Martyn began to wind down his introduction, wishing the audience luck before handing them over to the Chief Flying Instructor- a squat and serious man named Trevor Black.

'Oh, and by the way,' Martyn added, 'I am putting up a prize of ten thousand pounds for the first private pilot to win the top prize at the upcoming all-England Helicopter Championships. As you know, the field was totally dominated by military trained pilots until last year when our very own Trevor Black became the first civilian pilot to win it. This year Trevor is standing down to give us amateurs a chance. I myself will be entering, as I hope will many of you. To me this is a perfect opportunity to show the world that not only do Skyforce sell the best helicopters, but we also produce the best pilots.'

The statement was greeted with enthusiastic applause as Martyn left the room, exchanging smiles and nods with various members of the audience. Steve gave a wry smile, impressed at Shade's flair for self-promotion.

He turned his attention back to Valerie, who was bent studiously over an electronic organiser. She looked up and smiled apologetically.

'I'm afraid Martyn will be tied up until lunch, something's come up in personnel. Do you mind if I show you around?'

Steve smiled broadly. 'Not at all.'

They left the training school and made their way into the hangar itself, which housed the biggest helicopter workshop in Europe. It was practically full to the brim with machines, several brand new choppers fresh in from America stood waiting for full-assembly, looking strange without their characteristic thirty-foot rotor blades. Steve counted at least thirty mechanics all engaged with fifty-hour checks, annual certificate maintenance, or, with some of the older machines, the renewed three year CAA approved Certificate of Airworthiness. He couldn't help but feel impressed. The hangar was immaculate, the floor gleaming, everything you'd expect if you were going to invest a quarter of a million dollars on a helicopter.

Val's beeper sounded over the hubbub of the workshop. She sighed. 'Would you excuse me, Steve, the caterer wants my supervision on the layout of the buffet.' She smiled. 'I sometimes think this place would fall down without me.'

Steve returned the smile. 'It's no problem. Would you mind if I took a look around by myself?'

'That's fine. No one's flying at the moment, but keep clear of the active runway just in case.'

Val walked away, her head bent over her palm-pilot. Steve was once again conscious of staring at her. He reflected that Martyn Shade was a fortunate man; rich, young and sharing his bed with one of the most imposingly beautiful women Steve had ever seen. He smiled to himself and resumed his tour of the premises, walking through the hangar door and out onto the airfield. It was a pleasantly sunny morning he walked into and he was glad to see that the warm weather trend was keeping up, but there was just enough of a breeze to remind him of the capricious nature of English spring time.

He carried on walking to the old World War II hangar that housed Helispech GB. He was curious to see how the two companies measured up against each other. Needless to say, the inside of the Helispech hangar was a far cry from the Skyforce workshop. For a start, it was almost empty, housing only a few old machines including an old Hughes helicopter that looked as if it had come straight out of the Vietnam War. The hangar had an almost deserted feel, and not just because of the lack of any attending staff- dust had been allowed to pile up in corners, and machine parts sat in seemingly random piles.

Dominating the centre of the hangar was an Augusta 109 executive helicopter, a bold 'English Steel' logo emblazoned across the fuselage. Compared to the rest of the haggard machinery in the Helispech hangar, the Augusta gleamed through careful and meticulous maintenance. Steve thought it looked somehow proud in the low light, like a retired prizefighter who was still in great condition.

'Beautiful, isn't it?'

Steve turned at the sudden sound of the female voice, reverberating around the hangar. He squinted through the half-light.

'Val?' he said.

'Close, but no cigar,' came the reply. 'I'm Val's sister, Marnie.'

Steve couldn't believe his eyes. He had known that Val had a twin, but the similarities were remarkable. The same features and figure and the same styled hair. The only discernible difference was the manner of dress; far from Val's provocatively tailored suit, Marnie favoured a sombre casual look, with tight black jeans and a shoulder cut black shirt walking on top of black suede knee-high boots.

'I'm Steve. Steve Allen.'

'Well, Mr. Allen, what can I do for you?'

It had been felt by both his CO and Martyn Shade that the eminent arrival of a Royal should be kept on a 'need to know' basis, just as a precaution, so Steve had thought it prudent to fabricate a simple background and objective for himself in order to alleviate any suspicion of his true purpose at Skyforce. The cover was simple.

'I'm looking to buy a helicopter,' he said, feeling slightly foolish.

Marnie gave a wry half-smile. 'You want Skyforce next door if its sales you're interested in. As you can see we have a rather select clientele.' She gestured around at the mostly empty hangar.

Steve rubbed the back of his neck in a convincing display of awkwardness. 'Actually I was looking for some independent advice. I recently came into some money, and I've always wanted to own a chopper, but, to be honest, I don't really know that much about them.'

Marnie raised an eyebrow and Steve realised that there was another key difference between the two sisters- while Val's eyes were full of a penetrating suggestiveness, Marnie just seemed to convey an aura of amused impatience. Steve continued, undeterred.

'For instance, what's the difference between this English Steel copter and a Skyforce model?'

Twenty minutes later, sipping coffee from a chipped mug, he began to wish he'd never asked. Apparently the 109 had two turbine jet engines, while the Skyforce had only one conventional piston engine. The seating and payload capacity of the 109 was greater, but the Skyforce was more economical to run. And so it went on. Steve had lost interest in the subject matter fairly quickly, but he had no such qualm with the company. Marnie's easy-going approach to the conversation had revealed a sharp mind and a healthy whit, a combination he found particularly appealing.

The conversation gradually lilted from the technical to the social. 'So, where are you from, Steve?' Marnie asked.

'Originally from Ryde on the Isle of Wight, but staying in London these days.'

Marnie smiled. 'Quite a drive to talk shop. Are you only here for the day?'

'No, I'm staying at Rambleton Hall until the end of the week.'

'Very nice,' Marnie said, raising her brow. 'I've never been, but I hear the restaurant there is excellent.'

Steve smiled broadly, sensing the question hidden within the statement. 'You could have dinner with me there tonight, if you liked? You could educate me further in the mysterious world of helicopters.'

'Sounds good,' said Marnie. 'On one condition, though,' she added.

Steve arched an eyebrow expectantly.

'I'm due to flight test the 109 at some point today, so why don't I fly you down to Rambleton Hall and then stay for dinner?'

'That would be brilliant,' said Steve.

'Meet me here at six, I've got a lot to sort out in the mean time.'

'Will do.' Steve said. 'I'll look forward to it,' he added.

He watched her as she disappeared to the far end of the hangar, and then, with a spring in his step, made his way to the exit. He stopped short as something caught his attention on the ceiling. There was a long stretch of frayed rope still attached to one of the rafters, swaying ominously in the slight breeze. He couldn't help but shudder as he remembered Alan Johnston's method of suicide.

But surely they would have taken that down? He thought. Especially with his daughter still working here.

Steve dismissed his musings and left the hangar, his good mood blackened slightly by the disquieting memento of Alan Johnston's death.

On his return to Skyforce HQ, he was told that Mr. Shade was waiting to take him to lunch and was shown out onto the airfield where the English Steel MD was waiting with poorly concealed impatience. Martyn gestured Steve to accompany him, and they fell into a quick stride together as they walked toward an awaiting Two plus Two.

'Good afternoon, Steve,' said Martyn. 'Nile's has told me all about you.'

Steve frowned slightly. The referral to his CO by his first name was a clear intimidation attempt, meant to remind Steve of his place on the ladder. 'Unfortunately the government restricts him from telling you the good bits,' he replied, with just a sly enough hint of smugness to let Martyn know that he was a professional, there to do a job, and that he wasn't going to be impressed into blind subservience.

The taller man spoke again. 'I thought I'd give you a quick demo on the Two plus Two copter, thought we could fly somewhere for lunch.' Martyn talked as though he had other things on his mind.

'We aren't staying for the buffet then?'

'No, that muck's alright for the punters. I'll take us somewhere decent to eat, where we can get a drink or two.' Shade winked conspiratorially as he said this.

Steve wondered if the man was seriously going to fly a helicopter under the influence of alcohol. Wasn't there an old aircrew rule he had heard about? Eight hours between bottle and throttle? Steve tried not to let his first impressions colour his judgment, but he was beginning to believe that Martyn was a total prat.

As devil-may-care as Shade appeared, he was utterly thorough with his pre-flight inspection. Steve smiled at the helicopter's registration. Golf Oscar Sierra Kilo Yankee: GO-SKY.

As Martyn checked the oil, he asked Steve to sit in the left hand front seat, make himself comfortable and put the already in place headphones on. Steve did as he was bade, and a few minutes after starting the engine the helicopter was heading west towards Northampton.

'I've booked a table at the Swallow hotel. The food is good and they have a private heli-pad.'

Martyn went on to chat idly, explaining that the beauty of owning a helicopter was that you could land pretty much anywhere in the UK, providing you had prior permission. As he talked, he kept the copter flying at a low level on the outskirts of town, and Steve enjoyed the speed and handling and the casual grace with which Martyn piloted the machine. It seemed like only minutes before they were over the hotel and began descending down to the clear white 'H' at the rear.

Lunch was a strain. Steve had never been enamoured with a la carte dining, and he had been quietly amazed as Martyn polished off a full bottle of wine with his meal. Conversation wasn't a problem, though, as the Skyforce executive clearly seemed to relish the sound of his own voice. Steve had managed to butt in a few times, mentioning that he been over to view the English Steel hangar. Martyn had fallen quiet at that remark.

'You may as well know now, Steve, that my brothers and I don't really get on that well,' he had said.

Steve kept quiet, unwilling to divulge the extent of his research on Martyn's personal and family life. He had even read that each Shade brother took along his own solicitor to company board meetings. He couldn't fathom it. True, he and his own brother rarely spoke, but when Chris was on leave from his posting in Northern Ireland, they always made time to go for a drink together and catch up. He smiled to himself as he had a brief and absurd notion to take a solicitor with him the next time they met up…

On the flight back from lunch Martyn decided to show off. Steve wasn't sure if it was the wine, or simply Shade's natural obnoxiousness, but when the helicopter started to do steeper and faster turns, he couldn't help thinking that the man was deliberately trying to upset him.

'I'll show you what she can really do!' Martyn shouted into his headset microphone.

As soon as he spoke the helicopter pitched up, climbed steeply and then fell away sharply at tremendous speed. Steve hadn't been happy with the dangerous flying, and was relieved when Martyn decided to demonstrate the climbing rate and maximum ceiling of the machine. At least then the machine was in a stable climb.

'How high can it fly?' he asked.

'It can hover, out of ground effect, at twelve thousand feet and can cruise at fifteen thousand feet. Let's see if we can get up there shall we?'

The altimeter was already indicating that they were passing ten thousand feet.

'Won't we be needing oxygen soon?' asked Steve, calmly.

'We should be alright up to fifteen thousand feet, but, if you want to play on the safe side…"

Martyn showed Steve how to clip the oxygen mask around his face whilst he attached his own.

Steve couldn't help but think back to one of his old cases. Two American pilots in F11 jets had been cruising at twenty thousand feet when one of them thought it would be funny to 'moon' the other. Unfortunately, to bare his arse against the cockpit window it meant he had to remove his flight suit and, while his mate had laughed away, he had lost consciousness before he could reconnect his oxygen. His friend's laughter had turned to shouts of horror as the F11 turned on its back and crashed into the North Sea. They had searched for a week, but found no sign of the wreckage. It had been a poignant example against pissing about while in charge of an air craft-one that he felt Martyn could have benefited from.

The helicopter levelled off at fifteen thousand feet. Martyn switched on the auto-pilot and looked across at Steve. 'Look! No hands, piece of piss. Let's just enjoy the view shall we?'

Steve took the time to take a proper look at the helicopter he was riding in. The Two plus Two had proved itself a lovely machine, and because this was Shade's personal copter, it was fitted with all the extras: Connolly hide upholstery, fitted MP3 player, air conditioning. He looked across at Martyn, thinking again how lucky the man was. It was then he noticed something that made his heart race. Martyn's head was slumped against his chest, the tips of his fingers turning blue.

Steve had been in a lot of tricky situations in his time in the SAS, but he couldn't help the rush of panic as he realised he was flying thousands of feet in the air in an un-manned helicopter. He remembered an old trick he had been taught by a test-pilot once- in an emergency, the first thing you did was sit on your hands. He felt a bit stupid as he put his hands under his bottom, but even this simple action helped to clear his head of panic. Now he could begin to think straight again.

It was obvious that Martyn was suffering from oxygen loss, and that the helicopter needed to be brought back down to ten thousand feet where the oxygen system in the Skyforce wouldn't be required. He knew that the autopilot was still operating, so he gingerly reached for the cyclic control and eased it forward. This pitched the nose forward and the helicopter descended, picking up speed as it dropped down. The airspeed indicator climbed into the red and Steve was forced to ease back and let go of the cyclic control. The autopilot resumed control, but the helicopter had only lost a thousand feet. They were still too high.

Steve briefly thought of changing masks with Martyn, but if there was a fault with Martyn's oxygen mask, then Steve might black out before he even knew if Martyn had recovered, which would mean they would both fall unconscious and eventually die, flying until the helicopter ran out of fuel and crashed. In a brief instant, he remembered how a similar incident had resulted in the death of an American pop-singer and her entourage.

A cold sweat had formed on Steve's brow as he reached over and once again took hold of the cyclic control column. He estimated that if he kept the altimeter showing two thousand feet per minute descent rate then the airspeed would remain hovering just under the red arc. The helicopter began to vibrate heavily as it made its descent, but Steve pressed on. He had to get Martyn breathing oxygen before he suffocated, if not he would be forced to land the helicopter on his own- something he was sure would result in a messy death.

It seemed like hours before the altimeter swung around to indicate they were now at ten thousand feet. Steve glanced at Martyn's face and noticed the slight discolouration of his lips.

Christ, what if he's dead already? He thought, *How the hell am I going to get out of this?*

He thought about pressing the radio's transmit button and putting out a mayday call, but didn't really see what good it would do. He looked down again at the instrument panel and realised the helicopter was passing under five thousand feet.

'What happened? Did I fall asleep?' said Martyn, blearily.

Steve was torn between the urge to break the man's nose and kiss him on the lips. Instead he spoke calmly through gritted teeth. 'Too much wine with your meal, possibly.'

Martyn blinked, coming around quickly. 'No, no way. I've just been working too hard that's all. What's going on? That's Daventry radio mast up ahead, I didn't think I was this much off course.'

Steve refrained from commenting as Martyn turned off the autopilot, lowered the collective lever and commenced a slow easterly turn back to Bromsfield.

As they flew back, Steve turned the situation over in his mind. Years of air accident investigations had given him something of a sixth sense. If Martyn's blackout had been caused by a malfunction in the oxygen system, then surely both the pilot and the passenger would have been affected. He kept his suspicions to himself for the time being, waiting for an opportunity to check a few things over once they were safely on the ground. His gut instinct was telling him that the pilot's face-mask had been tampered with, which meant that somebody had wanted Martyn Shade dead. After dining with the man, he could see why…

Of course, the other possibility was that somebody had wanted Steve Allen dead, and that would mean that his investigation was more common knowledge than he had been lead to believe. He found either possibility daunting, but decided to allay his fears pending further investigation.

After they had successfully landed, Val walked out to meet them, arms and hips swaying rhythmically as her heels clicked on the concrete.

Martyn stepped out of the copter. 'Val, could you take Steve to meet Trevor and the rest of the instructors? Thanks.'

And with that, he climbed into the awaiting deep red Bentley turbo and drove off without so much as a goodbye. Steve was puzzled at the man's attitude; he had seemed largely unperturbed by his accident. He walked towards the hangar with Val in silence and then snapped his fingers in mock frustration.

'Damn, I left my wallet back there. Do you mind if I go back and get it?' he said.

Val looked down once more at her organiser. 'No that's fine. Just catch up with me at the training school.' Val walked away, leaving Steve free to investigate the chopper.

After walking back to the helicopter, Steve opened the pilot's door on the machine and inspected the face-mask. It didn't take long. All he did was pull the connecting tube away from the mask, look inside it, and there it was; a small, round yellowish coloured object. He squeezed the object out and brought it up to his nose. Detecting no scent, he tasted it and placed it immediately. It was a piece of sweet-corn. Steve had to admire the simple genius of it; after all, the sweet-corn had successfully blocked the oxygen flow to the pilot, and had they crashed it likely would have remained undetected in the resulting wreckage. The crash would have gone under the usual heading of 'pilot error' and nobody would have been the wiser.

Steve gave an involuntary shudder on his way back to the training school. It might have been from the sudden chill as the sun departed the late afternoon skies, or it might have been due to the fact that Steve was now up against a killer. And that he had no idea who that killer might be.

THE SEDUCTION

Standing under the warming torrent of the hotel room's power shower, Steve Allen's stomach grumbled with both hunger and nervous anticipation. Lunch now seemed like hours ago, which accounted for his hunger, and the fact that Marnie Johnson would be awaiting him in the bar downstairs accounted for his nervousness. The ex-SAS man smiled to himself. It had been a long while since he'd been nervous about a date, but then, it had been a long while since he'd had a date- especially with a woman of Marnie's calibre.

He had arrived at the Helispech hangar just shy of six o' clock. The Augusta 109 was waiting outside, prepped and ready to fly, with Marnie already in the pilot's seat waving Steve to come aboard. He had opened the door, adjusted and fastened his safety belt and donned his headphones before turning to greet Marnie. When he had, he had stopped short, mouth hanging limply. For some reason he'd assumed she would be decked out in her causal clothes from earlier, but she had dressed to the nine's, wearing a black silk dress that seemed to flow around her figure, the hem of which rode up on the pilot's seat to reveal stockings of equally dark and hugging material, and just a hint of delicate cream thigh. The only thing she hadn't changed were her boots, which seemed jarringly practical compared to the rest of her outfit. He watched her as she went through her checklist, blue eyes hunting, the tip of a pink tongue held up against her teeth in concentration. She was stunning. Steve shook himself free of infatuation. He was staring again, and the last thing he needed in the front of a helicopter was an erection.

Marnie had finished her checks, and gave him a friendly smile as the Augusta's rotors became invisible with speed. The gentle whisper of the Allison C120 turbine jet engine had increased to a powerful whine as they lifted off and headed north for Rambleton Hall.

Steve finished his shower and dressed for dinner. He was conscious of not wearing a tie as he entered the lounge bar. It seemed to be one of those bars where everybody was wearing a tie. He saw Marnie at the far end of the bar, sipping on a Martini Bianco and chatting casually to the maitre d'. The whole ambience of the extremely posh bar made Steve mindful of his working class roots, so he ordered a pint of lager before he sat down with Marnie.

'So what did you think of the Augusta 109?' was the first thing she said.

'Smooth. Very smooth. How much does a model like that cost?'

'That particular model with the full spec cost English Steel just over a million American dollars.'

Steve whistled through his teeth. 'I can see why. I never knew there was so much difference between the models, but comparing that with the Two plus Two is like comparing a Rolls Royce with a Vauxhall Vectra.'

Marnie laughed. 'You got to go up in one then?'

'Yes, I went up in Martyn Shade's personal machine. He piloted it himself.'

Steve caught himself searching for a reaction in Marnie's face. There was none, she remained politely attentive. Steve cursed the natural investigator in him, if he couldn't switch off his professional paranoia for a date with a beautiful woman, then when could he?

He continued. 'We had lunch at the Swallow Hotel in Northampton.'

'And how was it?' asked Marnie.

Steve grinned. 'Well if the Swallow was the Vauxhall Vectra then lets hope tonight's meal is the Rolls Royce.'

They both laughed as the maitre d' escorted them to their table.

Rambleton Hall was no disappointment. The meal was absolutely superb; fully justifying the two hundred pound charge, although Steve was glad Skyforce UK would be paying the bill.

Lets just call it quits for saving your life this afternoon, Martyn, thought Steve, smiling slyly.

The conversation was almost entirely professional throughout the meal, Marnie mostly talking about helicopters and helicopter related matters. Steve did his best to keep up his end of the conversation, but to be honest, there didn't seem to be anything Marnie didn't already know about aviation. Over coffee, Steve talked about his day at Skyforce, keeping up the pretence of a wealthy prospective customer.

'I've been invited to attend the final day of Skyforce's European safety course tomorrow. Apparently is held at RAF Cottesbrooke, where they handle the air traffic radar service.'

Marnie's eyes lit up. 'Not just that,' she said. 'It's a fully operational Tornado base.'

'Really?' Steve feigned surprise, though he had thoroughly researched the area as part of his case background.

'Oh, yes. It's the training centre for all of NATO's Tornados. Pilot's go there from all over Europe. That's sort of why they handle the civilian air traffic radio there- if there's one thing that a Mach 1 770mh Tornado and a Skyforce Two plus Two have in common its that they both tend to fly low-level.'

'Meaning?'

'Well, that there's always a chance of collision. That's why the RAF invites all new pilots to attend and see what they do. It sort of puts a face to the voice we speak to on radio, gives us a better understanding of the aviation 'community', so to speak.'

'Well, I shall look forward to it,' said Steve.

Marnie grinned. 'If you can, see if you can get them to let you sit in a Tornado cockpit. It's well worth it.'

Steve laughed. 'Every little boy's dream, I'm sure.'

Marnie was turning out to be fantastic company as well as fantastic looking and Steve was really enjoying himself. It was only when he asked how she managed to run Helispech GB almost single-handedly did a frown appear on Marnie's face.

'My father died recently. He was very well insured, so the company's debts were paid off. Otherwise Helispech would have been put into liquidation.'

'What about the rest of your family? Your mother?'

'She died in a mountain accident in Switzerland when I was just twelve,' answered Marnie, her eyes lowering to the table.

Steve cursed himself for putting his foot in his mouth. 'I'm sorry,' he said.

Marnie gave a brief and regretful smile. 'So am I. She was a wonderful woman.'

They each turned back to their coffees, the conversation weighted under the sudden change of mood.

'It's getting dark outside, you know,' said Steve, changing the subject. 'Will you be alright to get back? Are you able to fly in the dark?'

Marnie looked up into Steve's eyes, revealing a playful mischief, all of her sudden melancholy seemingly forgotten. 'Well, yes and no. Yes, I can fly in the dark, but no, I don't think I'll be getting back alright.'

Steve raised an eyebrow. 'How's that?'

Marnie smiled with mock demure. 'I thought I might stay with you tonight.'

*

Steve had led an adventurous life, his army career taking him to places he might never have seen in a normal day-to-day job. And in his youth, the best part about visiting new and interesting places was meeting new and interesting women. He had had plenty of sex; great sex, quick sex, casual sex, disappointing sex, even professional sex, but nothing could have compared with Marnie.

As soon as they had entered his room, Marnie stepped out of her dress, letting it fall to the floor with a silken whisper. She stood before him, naked bar the stockings and suspenders. Her body was firm and sculptured in the blue light of the moon, her mounds and crevices picked out in delicate extremes of light and shadow. She kissed him, tenderly at first, but with increasing waves of animal passion.

Steve could only stand dumb-founded as she took the initiative, shoving him back onto the bed and ripping open his jeans, revealing a penis erect to the point of aching. She mounted him, swaying her body in smooth, quick movements. Steve's neck jerked his head back at the startling pleasure as he fought desperately to stay in control. There was a sudden explosion of ecstasy in his head and lower body as he spent, unable to help himself. Marnie barely noticed, but continued her lithe movements and quick rhythm, working her way into a frenzy until she climaxed, her nails digging into Steve's chest, her blonde hair thrown back, her breasts jutting out as her spine arched. Steve could only watch her in rapt awe as the shuddering in her body eventually subsided.

The whole process was repeated three times before Steve began to drift off to sleep, exhausted and sweating. Marnie left without a word, just a gentle kiss after she had dressed herself.

He lay there in the dark, listening to the sound of an Augusta 109 heading toward to Bromsfield, and reflected that, right here and now, he felt luckier than Martyn Shade.

As he began to fall into a deep sleep, a particular thought struck him. Marnie hadn't mentioned her twin sister even once all night.

THE AIRBASE VISIT

Steve awoke early the next day, but felt little need for exercise after the previous night. He caught his reflection in the bathroom mirror as he brushed his teeth and realised he was still smiling. He would have to cut that out, he looked like some giddy schoolboy. And he couldn't allow himself to be distracted. After all, what had started as a routine investigation had taken on more sinister angles since yesterday's incident in Shade's Two plus Two.

He decided to refocus his mind on his job by looking over his notes for the upcoming Airbase visit. He had used the secure internet connection on his Mac Powerbook to request information from a designated Ministry Of Defence contact, in particular some further details on the list of members for the Helicopter Club of England. He had tried to narrow down the list to existing Skyforce UK customers, but, so popular were the firm, that the omissions were far outweighed by the remainders. There was even a member who flew all the way from Bournemouth to have his copter serviced at Skyforce.

He had also requested a list of those who used the Skyforce hangar for local needs, such as refuelling and oil. The full background check had listed only fourteen people, including Martyn Shade and the MP Rupert

Cooksley. Interestingly enough, there were two members whose background checks both cited criminal records; one Douglas Williams, a nightclub owner with two counts of ABH, and John James, a garage proprietor who, apart from dealing in second hand cars, had once been caught dealing speed. Apparently he had gotten away with a simple possession charge by pleading guilty, and was ordered to pay a heavy fine rather than given a prison sentence. Although these were hardly crimes that indicated predisposition toward sabotage and attempted murder, he thought he had best keep an eye out for the two characters, just in case.

Steve drove the twenty miles to the RAF base, his Lexus keeping a steady 55mph in cruise control, the weather holding clement over the wide midlands skies. His thoughts were troubling as he glided across the back roads- clearly someone wasn't happy with Martyn Shade, but what if the grudge was against the entire Skyforce UK setup? That would certainly complicate things from a security point of view.

With only a couple of miles to go, Steve noticed a sign for the run off to Barnwell Lodge. He recalled that this was the 'fly in' spot for all the visiting pilots visiting the RAF base, and that Val was going to be there to meet and greet the Skyforce customers. Steve decided to turn off and meet them there instead of waiting at the base. He drove down a narrow road way through wide green gardens and parked his car near the splendidly kept lodge, a mix of hearty brown stone work and Tudor style framings. He was just making his way towards the reception when Val came out to greet him.

'Hi, Steve, do you fancy some breakfast?'

Steve felt a slight surge of guilt seeing the woman who looked so much like Marnie, recalling her naked body and wondering just how identical the two sisters were. He mentally shook himself free of distracting thoughts and focused on the job at hand.

'Breakfast sounds great, thanks,' he said.

They walked through the reception area and lounge bar into the rear gardens, where a marquee had been set up to serve bucks fizz and croissants. Steve was briefly glad of the bacon and eggs he had had early that morning back at Rambleton Hall. All on the expense account of course...

'I'll leave you to mingle,' said Val, moving off as she spotted another guest arriving.

Steve took a walk through the tent and out the other side and stopped short at the view before him, in the fields behind the lodge a temporary wind sock had been erected, next to which there were thirty or so Skyforce helicopters lined up in neat rows, glinting glamorously in the sun. Steve smirked to himself as he was put in mind of some uncanny helicopter garden, and then a face he recognised caught his attention. It was the MP, Rupert Cooksley, looking as expensively preserved against age as he had appeared in his photos. Steve approached.

'Good morning. Rupert Cooksley, isn't it? I'm Steve Allen, pleased to meet you.'

Rupert was clearly trying to place Steve, but his faced glazed over to a politician's smile as they shook hands.

'Charmed, I'm sure,' he said.

Steve tried to hide a smirk. He didn't think people

actually said that outside of period dramas.

'Listen, what are your thoughts on the Two plus Two? I'm thinking of buying one myself, and I'd appreciate any advice you might have?' he said.

Rupert appeared to be eager to be elsewhere, edging slowly away as he prepared an excuse.

'You are, after all, one of the more famous Two plus Two pilots.' Steve continued, oiling his words around the axle of Cooksley's ego.

The change in the man was immediate. Steve never ceased to be impressed with how easily some people were won over with flattery.

They talked for five minutes, mostly about copter specs, but with some hint to Cooksley's private life. Steve reflected that the man was outwardly charming but also quite guarded in the way that he deflected any questions that might prove too personal. In short, he talked like a politician. But there were other things, like the way he carried himself, and a light inflection in his words that seemed to grate against the media image of the stolid rustic family man.

It didn't occur to Steve until Rupert was walking away that the MP was gay. He hid it well, but Steve was almost certain. Although perfectly harmless, Steve couldn't help wondering, if he can hide the fact that he is gay from the world, what else might he be hiding?

He put his musings aside for the time being. After all, politicians who lied about their private lives were nothing new, and his deceit was hardly indicative of a cold-blooded killer.

At that moment they were called to board the three army minibuses that would take them to the RAF base. The bus was mostly full when Steve got on, but he found himself a seat near the back with two other men. They talked and laughed loudly in the manner of people who had helped themselves to rather a lot of champagne at breakfast.

The minibuses' loud diesel engine spluttered into life, causing the whole cab to shudder wildly.

One of the two men nudged the other. 'Hey, Johnny-boy, I don't suppose they got this heap from one of your garages did they?'

The other man laughed, and poked his finger through one of the various holes in the seating upholstery. 'I don't know, mate- but it looks like they've nicked the seats out of your nightclub.'

As the men continued to take the piss out of each other, Steve thought back to his case file. These two men were apparently the nightclub owner and garage proprietor he had researched earlier that day. It was a stroke of luck that he had sat next to them. He leaned over and introduced himself.

'Hi, lads. Steve Allen.'

The nearest man, portly, balding and decked-out in casual golf-wear, shook his hand. 'I'm Doug.'

The other man- likewise portly with bright, grey hair- waved casually from his window seat. 'John James, pleased to meet you,' he said.

Steve opened with what he thought was a fairly safe conversation-starter considering the circumstances. 'So, are you guys helicopter pilots then?'

'Yeah,' said John, 'We own a Two plus Two between us.'

'I'm thinking of getting one myself,' said Steve. 'That's why I'm here, really.'

'Well I'd recommended the Skyforce Two plus

Two,' said Doug, 'It hasn't given us any problems.'

'And how hard do they hit the pocket?' said Steve, grinning.

John leaned over conspiratorially. 'Take my advice, pal, and find yourself a rich sucker to split the cost with.' He winked and pointed his thumb at Doug.

He chatted with the pair all the way to the base, and was surprised to find that he was actually getting on quite well with them. For all that they looked like Tweedle Dum and Tweedle Dee, they laughed and joked like the quintessential boys at the back of the bus.

Eventually the minibus arrived, and the passengers alighted. Doug turned to Steve and handed him a business card with his number on it.

'I'm turning forty-five this Saturday, Steve, and we're having a fly-in barbecue. Bit of tennis, bit of food, that sort of thing. Most of the fly-boys should be there. Come down if you like, it should be good craic.'

Steve took the card and pocketed it. 'Thanks,' he said. 'I'll be there.'

He watched as the two men walked away. If anything else, the barbecue would be an excellent opportunity to garner some more in-depth background on some of the Skyforce customers. Besides that, it sounded like it might be a good time.

The RAF base was pretty much uniform to every over military base Steve Allen had seen, with the same squat hangars and buildings, and the same practical and temporary feel to the décor. He shuffled in with the res of the crowd, allowing himself to be herded along.

The visitors were split into two groups, one of

which would be given the tour to the air traffic control tower and the other of which would be taken to the Tornado hangar. They would then break for lunch, after which the two groups would swap over. Steve had been put into the air traffic group, and they made their way up the internal stairs to the top of the control tower. There were four controllers on duty, all female and all gathered around a large circular radar screen. One of the controllers, a matronly woman with tiny half-moon glasses, began the presentation, explaining that they had good radar coverage that day and pointing out several aircraft indicated by slow moving dots on the screen. Most of the aircraft were transponder equipped, transmitting a unique four-digit number that was displayed below each radar dot.

The controller continued her presentation. 'We spend most our time making sure each aircraft has a good separation distance to avoid mid-air collisions. The radar coverage is extremely sensitive, it can even pick up skydivers at Sibson airfield, but our job is made a lot easier by aircraft's carrying transponders, which makes them more easily identifiable to our radar system. Unfortunately, not all aircrafts carry transponders, such as gliders or hot air balloons. Some pilots even choose to fly non-radar, which, as you can imagine, makes our jobs more difficult...'

Steve had to agree; non-radio flying was asking for trouble. He'd seen some of the results himself. He concentrated as the controller continued speaking.

'These radar screens are imperative for discerning what occasional traffic is flying in the area, because the Tornado training is extremely intensive, both day and night. As you can probably guess, the last thing we want is one of you private pilots being surprised by one of our boys.'

There was a general murmur of laughter. One of the visitors raised his hand to ask a question.

'Don't the Tornados fly at specific times?'

The controller nodded her head. 'Well, yes and no. Because of complaints from resident we have to rotate our Tornado training times on a regular basis. So, while we fly to very specific windows, these windows are constantly varied for the sake of the locals.'

The man raised his hand again. 'What about when local airfields have big air shows? Doesn't that interfere with your timetable?'

'Good question,' said the controller, 'Obviously we have contingency plans. For example, next Monday the airbase in Dusseldorf, Germany, is due to fly a low cross channel training sortie with several visual reporting points, one of which is at he Battle of Naseby monument just north of Barton House at 10.00 hours. Now, as you know, Barton House is where they are holding the All-England Helicopter Championship this weekend, and more specifically, they will be holding their navigation competition on the Monday. So, obviously, we intend to keep both parties well clear of each other, as well as keeping occasional and regular traffic cleared. As you can see from this example, our radar service is not only imperative for our training to be carried out at high speeds and low levels, but it is also a valuable tool for private flyers.'

The lecture rounded off with more questions asked and answered until, eventually, they broke off for lunch in the canteen. After Steve had finished eating the mediocre meal, he went round to the bar, where most of the party had headed, including Martyn Shade himself, mingling and politicking with his clients. Steve wasn't surprised to see that Doug and John were already there, propping up the bar. They waved him over.

'Alright, lads,' he called, 'Did you get a shot in the Tornado cockpit then?'

John nodded enthusiastically, swallowing a mouth full of his pint before replying. 'I did, but this fat bugger couldn't fit in!' He jerked his thumb at Doug, who returned a reproachful glare before laughing and patting his ample stomach.

'What have I got to look forward to then?' asked Steve.

John smiled, a schoolboy glint of excitement in his eyes. 'They showed us the weapon systems, the lock-on target, the on-board computer and the infrared guidance system- very smart, makes flying at night brighter than during the day.'

Doug joined in with equal enthusiasm. 'The in-flight computer system was incredible. You just log your way points in, your height, which is usually as low as two-hundred and fifty feet, your cruise speed, and the bloody thing will hedgehop at nearly Mach 1 by itself. I tell you, I wouldn't mind a shot on one of them.'

'Yeah,' John jeered, 'If you could fit in it.'

Before Doug could reply there was a sudden cacophony of alarm bells, followed by an approaching wail of fire engines.

The booming voice of Martyn Shade cut clear through the noise. 'What the hell is that? A drill?'

Almost as soon as he had spoke the station

commander entered the room, the crowd fell silent. 'Gentlemen,' he said, 'This is not, I repeat, not, a drill. We think a Tornado has suffered a bird strike. One of its engines has gone and the pilot is attempting a forced landing on runway zero eight- the furthest runway from the tower. I must ask you all to remain here until further notice. Thank you.'

The commander left the room. For a while everyone stood in silence, and then, as one man, they moved to crowd around the glass patio door, scanning the skies for the stricken aircraft.

'I see it,' shouted Doug, suddenly. 'Eleven o' clock high!'

Steve saw it, his stomach churning as he saw the craft yawing and pitching dramatically on what should have been a straight in approach.

'He won't make it, he's going too fast,' came the voice of Martyn Shade.

Steve turned to look at him. The man didn't seem worried, he was standing with his arms folded, an almost smug expression on his face. Steve's dislike for the man increased ten-fold.

Two of the off duty RAF airmen began muttering to one another. 'The more speed he has the more control over his flying surfaces. There must be damage to his aerolons.'

Steve could see the sense in the statement, but even so, the Tornado looked awfully high as it approached the runway. As the plane tried to level out above the runway it was rocking and rolling and seemed sure to crash and burn, but somehow, whether through sheer luck or unbelievable skill, the pilot managed to level out the wings and cut his remaining engine, coming to settle on the runway lightly. The whole room erupted into a wild cheer.

Steve felt a wash of relief course through his body. He turned to one of the off-duty airmen. 'You people certainly know how to put on a show.'

The relieved pilot gave a chuckle, and then raised another cheer when he shouted. 'Drinks are on the house!'

*

Steve had left the celebrations early, heading back to Rambleton Hall for a lazy bath prior to a further nights work on the preparation of his report. His phone had rang before he had even got undressed. He found himself hoping it was Marnie, but it turned out to be Niles.

'Steve, were you anywhere near RAF Cottesbrooke today when there was an incident involving a Tornado?'

'Yes, sir, I was at the base being showed around with the rest of the Skyforce customers. The jet suffered a bird-strike, but the pilot managed to bring it down on one engine.'

'It was no bloody bird strike, Steve. We've just had conformation; the Tornado was flying low over Wales when it took out the rear rotor blade of a Bell 206 helicopter. They were checking on a possible leakage on a gas pipeline. The engineers didn't find feathers on the Tornado, they found shattered rotor blade.'

Steve felt his blood run cold. 'And the helicopter crew?'

'Both dead,' said Niles. 'The co-pilot was a newly

wed, and the pilot leaves a wife and three children behind.'

Steve fell silent, unsure of what to say. All of a sudden, the celebratory atmosphere he had left behind at the bar seemed perverse.

Niles continued. 'I want you to come down to Gatwick tomorrow and we'll go through what you have of your report so far. The last thing we want is the future King of England being blown out of the sky by some kraut in a Tornado.'

'Of course,' said Steve.

'And there's something else we need to discuss, Steve. It's best said in person.'

'Understood,' said Steve, and put the phone down in a daze.

Two things kept him awake that night; one was the thought of the helicopter pilots, doing their job one minute, spiralling towards a certain death the next. The other was the fact that his CO had called him 'Steve'-something he only did when he had bad news.

MICHAEL McCONNEL

Michael McConnell stooped over the pool table, cue balanced delicately in his hand, his formerly shaggy hair now cropped and dyed blonde. He studied the balls on the table for a while, planning his next shot. His opponent, a younger man with a shaven head, tapped his foot impatiently. 'Haven't got all night you know,' he said.

McConnell looked up from the table. 'Distract me again and you'll be surprised just how prothetic that statement is.'

The younger man frowned. 'Come again?' he said.

McConnell sighed. 'I said shut yer bleedin' mouth before I shove a cue ball in it.'

The man grinned and held his hands up in mock surrender. 'Steady on, granddad, no trouble here.'

McConnell grunted and took his shot. A ball was potted, another coming to rest a hairs breadth from the pocket. He nodded with satisfaction, handed the cue to his opponent, and then sat at the table and took a long draught from his pint.

Perhaps a more cautious fugitive would by now have gone to ground, or better still, left the country entirely, but McConnell was nothing if not confident. Besides, the pub he was currently laying low in was the kind of place where undue questions were more likely to result in a bottle 'round the head than any answers. It was the kind of dive where people kept their heads down and their mouths shut, and that suited him just fine.

He stood up as his opponent finished his shot and took the cue back. He tapped the wood thoughtfully in his hand as he examined the table. The younger man was just a few shots from winning. Catching up would be difficult at best.

'Right,' said McConnell.

He swung the cue so fast that no one, especially not his luckless opponent, had time to know what was going on. The cue smashed over the younger man's nose, driving him down to a bleeding, moaning heap on the floor. No sooner had this happened than McConnell had placed a bar stool over his prone victims chest. He sat on top of it, pinning the man to the ground, and as he did so he retrieved the broken half of the cue and jammed it lightly into the younger man's eye.

'Granddad, is it?' he said.

The man screamed. 'What? What the fuck?'

McConnell grinned, aware that every eye in the pub was on him, and fully aware that no one would lift a finger to stop him. His reputation had kept him untouchable in prison for years, but it looked like a few people on the outside world were going to need a reminder.

'Listen here, lad, while I dispense some wisdom on you, free of charge.' The big Irish man leaned in close to his victim's face, a thin sliver of spittle escaping between his gritted teeth. 'Have some fucking respect for yer elders.'

The young pool player's screech reached an ear-splitting new pitch as McConnell slowly twisted the pool cue.

*

Michael smiled to himself as he walked back to the Bed and Breakfast he was staying at. The cool air of the Irish night felt good on his skin. Freedom was still a novelty, and he was glad that he'd made contingency's for the hand-over that had gone array a few days ago.

However, he had not returned to the Ireland he knew. Things had changed, talks of peace and half-measures had weakened the men, the soldiers, he'd used to know. They'd betrayed themselves without even realising.

McConnell would never betray the cause. Times may change, but the cause didn't. Britain out of Ireland. As simple as that. He had sacrificed his youth for that simple ideal. He had sacrificed his fiancé. He had sacrificed his freedom. He would be damned if he gave in now.

What he needed to do was re-establish himself at the top of the hierarchy. There were plenty of IRA members, old and new, who'd rally to his command if he put his hat in the ring. But he'd need money first. Lots of money.

And after that? Something spectacular. Something that would leave no doubt that Michael McConnell was back on the scene and here to stay. Something that would top every stunt he'd ever pulled. And, this being

Michael McConnell, that would be a tall order indeed.

*

Steve had drove from Rambleton Hall to Gatwick in just under two hours, getting flashed twice by police speed cameras as he sped through restricted road works. Unable to sleep, he had left that morning at 5.00am, planning to have breakfast at HQ before Niles Bailey arrived. However, when he pulled into the staff car-park, he noted that his CO's ancient 60's Daimler was already there, so he went immediately to the office.

Niles had looked troubled and tired when he answered the door. 'Come in, Steve. Fancy a coffee?'

Steve declined and took a seat, the bulky printout of his report thus far held in a black plastic wallet.

Niles pinched the bridge of his nose. 'Before we start, Commander, just tell me one thing- these helicopters, are they safe?'

Steve waited. Obviously Niles was deeply troubled by something.

'The reason I ask is that I've been doing a bit of research myself. Only last month a Skyforce Two plus Two crashed in Australia when the main rotor blades failed in mid-air, for Christ's sake. It's not like in a light aircraft where if the propeller shatters you can still glide the thing and have a chance of survival. If you're in a helicopter and your main rotor fails, then you're dead. End of story. I mean, really, is this the sort of machine anyone should be flying, let alone a Royal?'

Steve tapped the plastic case in front of him, before

giving his response. 'When a Skyforce leaves the factory all of its components are given a specific time limit before they have to be overhauled or replaced. In the case of the main rotor blades its ten years or two thousand hours in the air, whichever comes first. The helicopter you're talking about was one of the early models, which have a history of bonding problems with the blades. Skyforce USA assures me that the newer models have titanium rotor blades, and they're over twice the strength of the old ones.'

Niles nodded, taking a large swig of his coffee. 'And you're happy with the engineering standards at Bromsfield?'

'They're immaculate,' Steve replied. 'All the mechanics are ex-RAF, the equipment is first class and everything's spotless. You could eat your dinner off the hangar floor.'

'And the instructors?'

'I've only really met Trevor Black, the Chief Flying Instructor. But if he's anything to go by then we've nothing to worry about. He's ex-RAF and recognised as one of the best pilots in the UK. He was the first civilian pilot to win the helicopter championship. I can look into the other instructors, but I should imagine that if the Prince will be taking instruction from anyone at Skyforce, it'll be the CFI.'

Niles nodded in agreement. He seemed distracted. 'What about Shade?'

'Driven, ruthless and confident to the point of arrogance. I'm keeping him in the dark about the sabotage on his oxygen mask, but to be honest, he doesn't seem particularly troubled about the incident.'

'Do you have any leads on the sabotage?'

Steve shook his head slowly. 'There were two men with criminal records present at the airfield that day. To be honest, I don't think they were involved, but I should be meeting them at a barbecue tomorrow. I'll make further assessment after I learn more about them.'

Niles stared into space for a moment before replying.

'Not to imply any lack of confidence in your abilities, Commander Allen, but do you think its time to involve the local police?'

Steve grinned. 'I wouldn't recommend it, sir. Not if we still want to keep a low profile. If police are crawling around the airfield it might compromise my evaluation.'

'Fair enough, fair enough. Anyone else caught your eye?'

Steve's thoughts automatically turned to the bits of Marnie that had caught his eye, but decided not to mention that to his boss.

'I've met pretty much all the major players there,' he said. 'The only person who's been absent is the chief engineer, Richard Jones. He's been in Florida for the past week, but should be back any day now. He's an ex-Helispech employee, but he's excelled in Skyforce. His leave of absence puts him out of the frame as far as the sabotage was concerned.'

Niles nodded, his thoughts still seemingly elsewhere.

'Was there anything else, sir?'

The CO was silent for a while. 'You remember Michael McConnell?'

Steve frowned in puzzlement. 'Of course, sir. It'd be

difficult not to.'

'He's absconded from prison.'

Steve felt a cold wave flow down his spine. 'How?' He said.

'Total balls-up. Sin Fein was under pressure to negotiate his release, but public opinion was too against it. He was due to be released, but it was all cancelled at the last minute.'

'But he escaped anyway?'

Niles nodded. 'Apparently he had made arrangements against just such an eventuality.'

'When?' Steve snapped.

'Three days ago.'

'And nobody thought to inform me?'

Niles levelled a cool gaze at Steve. 'No. We've been keeping the whole embarrassment very low profile, and frankly, Commander Allen, it's not your problem. M15 have things well in hand.'

'I should have been informed,' replied Steve, coldly.

Niles sighed. 'How old are you now, Steve? Wrong side of forty?'

Steve nodded.

'Your SAS days are over. You know as well as I do that you can never go back to that life. It's time to stop treating the CAA as a secondment and settle in for the long haul. I don't want you traipsing around the country looking for redundant IRA terrorists, I want your full attention focused on the Skyforce situation. Is that clear?'

'He's dangerous,' said Steve. 'You and I both know that the Real IRA are still very much active and a force to be reckoned with, despite the peace talks. Michael McConnell could turn out to be just as much a pain in the arse now as he was all those years ago.'

'That's as may be, but it isn't your problem anymore. You're good at what you do, Steve. You've turned into a solid fixture here at the CAA. Its time to put the past behind you.'

Steve's hand went unconsciously to his shoulder. His thoughts returned to the lifeless eyes of a dead seventeen-year-old girl.

'And if he comes looking for me?'

'Intelligence suggests that he left the country almost immediately after his escape.'

Steve was silent for while. 'I killed his fiancé. He hasn't forgotten that. He never will.'

'His fiancé was a terrorist, just like him. You were defending yourself,' said Niles.

Steve stared hard at his CO. 'So you don't think he's still after revenge?'

For a moment, Niles didn't say anything. Then he sighed, pinching at the bridge of his nose again. 'I'll tell you as soon as we have any information on his whereabouts, that's as much as I can do.'

Steve nodded his thanks.

'In the mean time you have a week to finish your report. The lad's father needs to know that everything is totally solid.'

Steve grinned at the way Niles referred to the future King of England as "The lad's father", but his good humour was short lived. On the way back to Rambleton Hall his mood turned black. Michael McConnell was free and, MI5 or not, Steve Allen would be sleeping with one eye open from now on.

THE DRUGS RUN

Rupert Cooksely had enjoyed his day at RAF Cottesbrooke. One of the few who had declined to sit in the Tornado cockpit, the excitement of the day had been enough for him. To be in the company of men was always a joy- but men in uniform; that was something special. He smiled to himself as he sat in front of his open fireplace, glass of brandy in hand, his wife sitting opposite him. He was an old letch, he knew, but here was something else he admired about the fly-boys other than the obvious. He had caught himself reliving the excitement of the Tornado incident to his wife over dinner, and had been surprised by how much he admired the skill and professionalism of the Tornado pilots.

He had been getting on well with Marie that day, she was always suspicious and disapproving of any time he spent away from home, and to be able to talk openly about something as healthy and boyish as aeroplanes was a refreshing change from their usual uncomfortable small talk. They were chatting about the latest piece of airfield gossip- that a Royal was to be learning to fly at Bromsfield- when a knock at the door had interrupted them.

'Bit late for visitors,' Marie had commented as she

got up to answer the door. She returned seconds later. 'It's for you, a man. I'll go upstairs out of the way.'

The look of quiet disgust she gave him was familiar by now, but what cost for happiness? Rupert reflected that he hadn't arranged anything for that evening as the visitor entered the room, he was tall and broad, with neatly cropped blond hair, tanned skin and dark sunglasses. Rupert had just enough time to reflect that the stranger wasn't really his type when a sudden certainty of dread settled in his chest.

The stranger spoke with an all too familiar Irish accent. 'I see your wife is accustomed to late night visitors.'

Rupert could barely speak. 'It's you.'

The big Irishman grinned. 'Michael McConnell at your service. Now sit down and shut the fuck up.'

'What do you want?' Rupert said. For a moment he was convinced that the man had come to kill him, to silence him as a potential witness.

'Simple, really. I want you and your helicopter. Now. Tonight.'

Rupert flustered. 'What for? Its dark, for Christ's sake! I'm not rated for night flying, I'm colour blind.'

McConnell didn't seem to be listening. He threw over a small note pad. 'Here are the co-ordinates for your navigation computer. We're flying to Holland.'

'But, I can't… I don't have enough fuel.'

Michael's face froze. 'I don't want you to lie to me ever again Rupert. I know for a fact that you have a fuel bowser in your hangar. If you fuck with me again, in any way, I will cut your dick off and force-feed it to you. Do you understand?'

Rupert was too shaken to reply.

'Now go and fuel up, I'll be out when I hear it start up.' McConnell helped himself to some brandy, standing casually as though he were a visiting relative.

Rupert got to his feet unsteadily and made his way to the door. He stopped as McConnell spoke again.

'Oh, and Rupert? If I hear sirens, your wife'll be first, then your son, and then you. So's you can watch, yeah?'

Rupert swallowed hard, fighting against the tears of panic that pressed against his eyes.

*

It took Cooksley nearly thirty minutes to prepare the Skyforce. First of all he had to hand pump over one hundred litres of fuel manually into the auxiliary fuel tank. Then he had to attach the tow wheels and push the copter well clear of the building before he could do all the necessary checks, input the computer and start the engine. The last thing he wanted to do was to try and explain what he was doing to his wife. God knew there were enough lies between them already.

McConnell came out of the house, bent low to avoid the rotors, and got in. Cooksley thanked providence for the clear weather; the half-moon made the night crisp and bright. Though his eye condition had always prevented him from officially completing the night flying course, he had illicitly flown at night enough to know that on a clear moonlit night, with all the towns lit up below, navigation was easier than during the day. So it was with good visibility and an accurate course, range and bearing from his computer that he took off and headed east.

Cooksley deliberately flew as low as possible with his electric transponder switched off so that he would not be picked up on radar. The last thing he wanted was to be classed as a 'runaway' and tracked down. He would fly the lunatic Irishman to Holland, do his best to get them both back, and hopefully that would be the last of it.

McConnell was silent for the journey, an old briefcase held steadily on his lap.

Everything went according to plan until they approached the Dutch coast. After they had left the English coastline the lights on the shore had been clearly visible. Now that they were approaching the Dutch coast there were no such lights. The entire coastline was obscured by cloud. Rupert swallowed hard, feeling a tight ball of anxiety build up in his abdomen. It was time to lose height and prepare to land, but he knew that at any minute he would be flying into cloud with no idea where he was, at what height and what he might be flying into. His left arm trembled as he lowered the collective lever. He bought the cyclic control column back reduced the engine power from twenty-two manifold pressure down to fifteen. The machine was now doing only sixty knots and was descending at five hundred feet per minute.

Cooksley kept his eyes glued to his instruments, making sure his slip and turn indicator remained central, that his artificial horizon indicator was straight and level, and that his speed and rate of decent were constant. This would all be quite routine work with a well-lit horizon for the eyes to lock on to, but soon it would be pitch black and he would have to rely on his instruments telling him things his own sense of balance might not necessarily agree with. He leaned over and switched his landing light on as he entered the cloud, but all this did was transform the blackness into an impenetrable grey. The sweat dripped from his forehead. His senses were telling him he was leaning to the left, but he had to trust his instruments. He forced himself to believe that they were right and his feelings wrong. He felt like a puppet on a string, like he was walking a tightrope blindfolded. If he lost it now he knew he would never regain control.

All of a sudden they were clear of the cloud. Rupert made an unintelligible noise in his throat as he realised they were heading toward a church spire with an illuminated clock in it. He managed to evade a near-certain collision by the skin of his teeth. He looked at his navigation computer and realised with intense relief that there was only two miles until their intended rendezvous point.

Rupert nearly jumped out of his skin as McConnell slapped his thigh. 'You see?' He said, laughing. 'Piece of piss.'

Cooksley neglected to tell him he'd just been part of an aviation miracle.

Suddenly something caught Michael's attention.

'There they are.' He said. 'That's the signal, those flashing lights.'

Cooksley flew towards the lights, which turned out to be a truck at the side of a deserted road. Cooksley once again thanked a god he didn't really believe in for the flat landscape of Holland. He was able to land near the truck with ease.

The big Irishman opened his door. 'Keep the engine running, I wont be long.' He said, and hopped out into the night.

Rupert looked anxiously at the fuel gauges. Just over half full. No problem getting back to England then, if the machine ran low he could stop near a service station and buy a few cans of petrol. It certainly wouldn't be the first time a pilot had done the same.

McConnell returned, throwing an old sports bag into the restricted space behind the pilot, and then climbed into the passenger seat and fastened his safety belt. He caught Rupert's questioning gaze.

'Twenty-five kilos of pure uncut cocaine,' he explained. 'Enough to turn a very pretty penny back in the UK.'

The Irishman was still laughing as the helicopter took off and headed west.

As Rupert flew back, he decided to once again hedgehop and keep below the clouds rather than risking fate by flying up through them. He was on good form as they reached the coast and started the North Sea crossing, skimming the waves with his landing light on at barely one hundred feet. He was just starting to feel relaxed when the low fuel light blinked on. The colour drained from his face.

'Oh fuck, no.'

'What's the matter?' said McConnell, all trace of his former good humour now evaporated.

'We must be flying into a strong head wind, all the fuel's nearly gone.'

'So what's the flashing light mean?'

'That we've only got enough fuel for five minutes flying, and we're already fifteen minutes out to sea. We'll have to prepare to ditch.'

McConnell began to laugh, dangerously. 'You're fucking kidding me, right?'

Rupert shook his head. 'We've no choice. We either brave the sea now or wait until we crash.'

McConnell laughed wildly. 'Fuck that!' he said.

Rupert was just about to bring the chopper into a hover at a safe distance above the water when he saw the two lights in the distance, one red and one green.

'Oh, thank Christ,' he murmured.

'What is it?'

'Up ahead, it's a ship.'

They flew onwards, the lights in the darkness getting closer. Rupert nearly laughed with relief.

'It's an oil tanker! They've got more room to land than most air fields!'

McConnell cuffed him around the head. 'Then what are you waiting for, idiot? Land the bastard thing!'

Cooksley bought the helicopter in to hover above the white 'H', and seconds after the skids had settled on the safety of the ship's deck, the engine spluttered and died. The rotor blades continued to spin, but the only sound was the hum of the master electrics. For a while the two of them just sat there, looking out to sea.

'Somebody up there likes me,' said Michael McConnell, eventually.

*

The next day they were docked at Felixstowe and, after Michael had bribed the captain with a couple of grand and a few bags of white powder, they were fuelled up and on their way back to Northamptonshire. It was mid-morning when they landed back at Rupert's farmhouse, and Rupert had just finished pushing the Two plus Two back into its hangar when he felt the press of cold steel in the nape of his neck. He spun around instinctively, only to realise that McConnell held a Beretta pistol levelled at his throat. He swallowed hard against the sudden taste of tin in his mouth.

'I don't understand,' he said.

Michael grinned amicably. 'It's quite simple, boyo. I've got no further use for you. And if you're useless, then you may as well be dead.'

He cocked the pistol and Rupert felt his knees give way. His mind turned white hot with panic, his mouth gaped open and shut like a fishes.

'No,' he said. 'No, wait.'

Michael shook his head with mock regret. 'Sorry, old timer.'

Rupert flinched as the barrel of the gun was forced under his chin. 'Surely there must be something? I'm a bloody MP surely there's some way I can be useful to you?' He spoke quickly, desperation giving his voice an eerie seriousness, as if he were brokering a deal rather than pleading for his life.

Michael put his hand on his hip, as though berating a particularly stupid child. 'How's that, then?'

'Information!' Rupert blurted.

'Information? What do you think this is, a bloody Bond movie?'

Rupert's brain went into overdrive as he desperately thought of some way to barter for his life. 'I have information that might prove useful to you! To the IRA!'

Michael sighed. 'Go on then. What?'

'The Prince, the heir to the throne; he's coming to Bromsfield to learn how to fly a helicopter.'

McConnell slowly put the gun away, a wicked grin cracking his face.

THE BARBECUE

Saturday turned out to be a perfect day for a barbecue, one of those rare days in May that were like the height of summer rather than the first days of spring. The sky was deep blue and cloudless as Steve drove from his hotel, across the county border to Leicestershire and the home of Doug Williams; nightclub owner, helicopter pilot, and possessor of a criminal record.

The music system in the Lexus belted out some Beatle's classics, a perfect counterpoint to Steve's darkened mood. Michael McConnell was loose, and, as much as he tried to concentrate on the job at hand, the Irishman's spectre was burnt solidly into the back of his mind, a dull anxiety that shadowed every thought. He always knew his past would catch up with him one day, but he couldn't think of a less convenient time than when he was working under the direct request of the Royal family.

The terrorist wasn't the only thing grabbing at his attention, though. He couldn't stop thinking about his night with Marnie- the perfect lines of her body, the taste of her mouth, the frenzy of her hair. Here was a girl that Steve hardly knew, but she had hooked him like no one before.

He'd never married, and to be honest had never

regretted it. In his younger days his need to live life on the edge had superseded the need to have a family of his own, and he had grown older with no qualms about his choice of lifestyle. He had a few women he could call on the visits back to his Camden flat, but he never wanted anything more out of them than a mutually good time with no pressure for relationships and commitment.

And then there was Marnie…

Steve grinned mirthlessly to himself. Mooning about like a love struck teenager could wait until he was off duty. He had a job to do.

Approaching a large roundabout he noticed a sign for Middleton, Doug's village. He set his mind on finding the right house, glad of the brief distraction from thoughts of love and vengeance.

The house wasn't difficult to find, a large and modern build with a front door festooned with balloons and far too many cars in the driveway. He noticed that one large and expensive looking 4X4 bore the license plate MAT 11N. Steve reflected that Doug must cook one hell of a burger for Martin Shade himself to be attending.

I wonder if he'll be there with his wife or his mistress, he thought. *I wouldn't be surprised if it was both. Arrogant bastard.*

He parked his car and made his way round to the back garden to reveal an acre of land littered with mismatched garden furniture and full of people. The smell of roasting meat filled the air and Steve wasn't surprised to see a hog roast had been set up next to a makeshift bar. He grinned. It was only early afternoon but it seemed the party was already in full swing.

'Hi Steve, glad you could make it!'

Steve barely had time to register who was talking before Doug was shaking him enthusiastically by the hand. Today the club owner was wearing a loud hula-shirt and a white panama hat. The slight whiff of rum on his breath completed the image of a man bent on celebration.

Doug turned around to the crowd and called. 'Hey everybody, this is Steve Allen; future pilot we hope!'

With that he let go of Steve's hand and gestured for him to join the company. Steve did so willingly, finding a drink in one hand and a pork roll in the other almost instantaneously.

I must admit, he thought. *I've had less enjoyable assignments.*

Just then Steve spied Val Johnson deep in conversation with an older woman. Val was dressed casually today, but even her casual wear had the air of a carefully constructed and presented uniform. It was a white summer dress, complimented by a loosely tied shawl of whispey material. She looked stunning yet approachable, and Steve guessed that she was just as much on duty as he was. He couldn't place the older woman, but something about her made him recall the hours of research on his personnel files.

His speculation was interrupted by the familiar rhythmical burr of an approaching helicopter. A nearby gazebo began to flap crazily as a Two plus Two came in to land at the back of the garden.

There came a familiar booming voice. 'Always nice to see one of my babies in action.'

Steve turned to see Martyn Shade, dressed in sports-wear and expensive sunglasses, staring rather too proudly at the landing chopper. His arm was placed casually around the woman Val had been talking too. Steve balked. The smug git really was arrogant enough to come to a barbecue with his wife and mistress. He made a mental note to try and talk with Mrs. Shade later in the day.

He tried to catch a glimpse of Val's expression, but couldn't see past Martyn. Steve wondered how the girl was feeling, to be here in a professional capacity as her lover socialised with his wife...

The Two plus Two landed safely at the back of the garden, revealing the pilot to be John James, who locked down the rotor blades before walking over to join the company. Doug was there waiting for him, a plate of food in hand.

'I'm surprised you didn't lose your fillings landing like that,' he joked.

John laughed. 'The Queen herself could have been sipping tea in the back during that landing and not spilled a drop.'

A brief pang of suspicion sounded in Steve's mind as he heard the causal mention of a Royal by the two people he was here to investigate. He dismissed it as coincidence, but decided to probe his hosts a little further. He walked over and made himself known.

'Hi,' said John, greeting him with the same friendly enthusiasm as Doug had earlier. 'Don't think I've forgotten about taking you up for a spin later. We'll do it after lunch okay?'

'Great, I'll look forward to it,' said Steve, still playing the role of a keen potential buyer.

Doug winked at him conspiratorially. 'If you're going up in the air with him, then I suggest you don't do it on a full stomach. Not unless you want to spoil your shoes.'

John raised two fingers in response. 'If you're so appalled with my flying, then why don't you fly at Barton this year and I'll navigate?'

'You two are entering the championships?' Steve interrupted.

'Oh, yeah,' said John. 'As long as there's ten grand up for grabs then it's worth a shot. Or it least it will be if I'm flying…'

'Will you be going, Steve?' asked Doug.

Steve nodded with well-acted enthusiasm.

'Good,' said Doug, and pointed at John. 'Then you can have a good laugh at this idiot's flying.'

Steve chuckled and went to get some more food, leaving the two friends to trade insults. While he was queuing up by the barbecue, three more Two plus Two's landed at the back of the garden. He didn't know the newcomers by name, but he recognised them from RAF Cottesbrooke.

'Mr. Allen?'

Steve turned around to see Val approaching with a party guest he had only ever seen in photographs. It was Richard Jones, the chief engineer at Skyforce. His pink, sunburned skin and the slight gold tint to his puffy grey hair was evidence of his recent stay in Florida.

'I don't believe you've met Richard Jones, our Chief Engineer.' Said Val. 'I thought that if you were still interested in buying a Two plus Two then there's no one more qualified to field your questions than Richard. Richard this is Steve Allen.'

Richard shook Steve's hand warmly and smiled,

revealing brilliant and obviously capped teeth.

'Hi,' said Richard. 'I'm just back from Skyforce in the states, so I can give you all the up-to-date information on the new model we're bringing out next year.'

Steve barely had time to return the greeting before the engineer began enthusiastically reeling off the specs for the new Skyforce model. Val walked away quietly as Steve was left to the bombardment of facts and figures- the Two plus Two's superior fuel economy over it's nearest rival, the turbine speed from its proven cyclonic piston engine. Steve reflected that before this assignment was over he was going to be an unwilling expert on helicopters. He eventually managed to interject with a question of his own.

'What about the safety record?'

Richard Jones waved a hand dismissively. 'Oh, there's been a few accidents, of course. It's the law of averages. When you're selling as many machines as we are there's bound to be a few hiccups. But it's almost always down to pilot error.'

Steve thought about the Bell 206 helicopter that had been obliterated by a Tornado over Wales, leaving widows and fatherless children in its wake. Is that what Jones would refer to as a 'hiccup'? His sudden dislike for the engineer made him forget about his pretence of naivety.

'What about the recent crash in Australia? The sheep farmer who's rotor blades disintegrated in mid flight?' he said.

Steve didn't know if he had spoken a little louder than normal, but there was lull in the surrounding conversation, as though his remark had caught the attention of a good number of the party guests.

Richard's eyes narrowed slightly, a glassy look came into his eye that might have been surprise or discomfort, or perhaps both. 'Those rotor blades were out of hours and the helicopter was well overdue a proper service. I'm sorry, but I didn't realise that was public knowledge yet, Skyforce have yet to release a statement. Can I ask how you heard about it?'

In the back of his mind, Steve felt a flush of irritation at himself. His anger had led him to jeopardise his cover. 'I'm sure I read about it in this months Helicopter World,' he lied.

Jones held his gaze a moments before mumbling an excuse and walking away, clearly disturbed by what Steve had told him. There was a brief uncomfortable silence, broken when Doug held up a glass and announced with mock grandeur:

'It just goes to show- one should never mix one's chopper with one's sheep.'

There were a few groans and a few laughs before everybody got back to their own conversations, with Steve's remarks hopefully forgotten.

He felt a hand on his shoulder and turned around to meet the broad grin of John James.

'If you still want that flight I promised you then we'd better go now before I have a drink.'

*

They flew around the village twice, which looked like somebody's hobby model, with its hills and farms and a rustic church spire. John's flying was smooth and careful, a far cry from Martyn Shade's recklessness and Marnie's sharp proficiency. While they flew, they talked idly about the pleasures of flying; the sense of freedom and potential that the clear skies offered, and the convenience of the Two plus Two's ability to land almost anywhere with a bit of space.

They landed back in the garden, John expertly squaring the skids almost exactly on the depressions they had left in the grass when he had landed the first time around. They were still talking as John switched the engine off and they waited for the rotor blades to stop turning.

'So, what made you decide to become a pilot?' asked Steve.

John froze, his hand still outstretched to turn the radio off, his grin sagging at the sides. For a moment Steve regretted asking the question and wondered if John would even reply. When he finally spoke, it was without the near constant joviality that normally coloured his tones.

'I learned to fly after my wife drowned at a naval base in Portland,' he said.

Steve didn't no what to say. 'I'm sorry,' he managed.

John shook his head. 'It was a good few years back, but when you lose someone, particularly in a sudden accident... well, it stays with you. It changes you.'

Steve nodded his head and said nothing.

John sighed and continued. 'I was on holiday in Weymouth with my wife Jenny and my Daughter, Angie. Angie was only young at the time, couldn't have been much more than six. I've always loved helicopters, so we took a trip down to Portland to see them flying. There were high winds that day and they were all grounded, so we walked along the promenade taking photos of all the machines lined up like a model collection. Jenny was patient, bless her. She never did share my enthusiasm that's for sure. She must have been bored out of her mind, but she never complained.' He smiled to himself in recollection, a smile that faded quickly.

'To this day I don't know what happened. One minute everything was fine, the next minute Angie was in the water, screaming. Like I said, the weather was bad and the seas were choppy, and there's Jenny taking off her shoes and shouting at me to get help. I felt like a useless prat. You see; I can't swim. I never learned. Never got around to it. So my wife dives in and saves our little girl while I'm on the promenade crying like an idiot. Jenny manages to pass Angie up and I drag her clear. I don't realise how cold the waters are until I hold my little girl and see that her lips have turned blue. And then, when I reach down to help my wife up, something happens.' John stopped a moment, his eyes far away.

'She's just carried away. Like the sea decided to keep her. She's swimming towards me but the waves just keep pulling her back. She doesn't even shout or scream- she's just got this look of determination on her face. God, she was a strong woman. Not strong enough though, she gets carried way out of my reach and I start to panic. It hits me and I run to the naval base and raise the alarm. It didn't do much good. There was a row of over twenty helicopters and no bloody pilots. By the time they had launched a boat out, Jenny had drowned.'

The two men sat in silence for a while, until John turned around, his former grin returned, but a painful sadness in his eyes.

'So you see, Steve, I did two things after that day. I learned to swim, and I learned to fly a helicopter.'

*

As Steve headed back to the barbecue he mentally crossed John and Doug off of his list of suspects for the attempted murder of Martyn Shade. After all, other than their criminal records, there was really no incriminating reason why they should want him dead, and his conversations with them had led him to believe that they were quite good-natured people- record or no record.

There were other, more obvious, suspects. Martyn's wife, perhaps; was she aware of the extent of the man's relationship with Val? If so, how did she feel about it? The same could be said for Val; was she tired of waiting in the wings for Martyn? Tired of the humiliation of being the other woman? And with no criminal record, could either of them be upset enough to do something so drastically out of character?

Steve knew he would have to keep a sharper eye out. If a threat existed to Martyn Shade within the Skyforce organisation, it would prove an unacceptable risk for a Royal, regardless of how personal the attack on Shade was.

After circulating among the guests and making polite conversation, Steve made his excuses, wished Doug a happy birthday, and returned to his car. He hadn't even got the keys in his ignition when he heard a tap on his window. He looked out into the stony face of Martyn Shade.

He wound his window down. 'Anything the matter?'

'Your gaff over the Australian incident has blown your cover with Richard Jones.' Martyn spat. 'He's our chief engineer and he's not stupid! He doesn't believe for a second that you're an interested buyer and he's demanding to know what's going on.'

Steve nodded calmly. 'Where is he now?'

'He's eating with the others, why?' Martyn said, frowning.

'Go and tell him I want to see him. Now.'

Martyn's mouth formed an 'o' of surprise that nearly made Steve laugh out loud. Clearly the man wasn't used to taking orders, but Steve had had enough of playing things Shade's way. Martyn left, and a few minute later a very sheepish looking Richard Jones approached. Steve beckoned him over to his window and spoke in low and forceful tones.

'My name is Steve Allen, but for your benefit, seeing as you're ex-RAF, my full title is Commander Steve Allen, on secondment from the special air services to the civil aviation authority. I am currently investigating Skyforce UK and all aspects of its line of business. I have been ordered to ensure that the engineering standards are of the highest possible and, as such, I will meet you in your office at nine o' clock Tuesday morning. I want a full rundown on all the personnel you employ, their background and qualifications, and most important of all, I want full access to your computer for a printout of your service and maintenance records.'

Steve didn't even wait for a reply. He just drove off,

revving his engine, his tires spinning slightly on the driveway. Richard Jones was left standing white faced and shell-shocked.

As he drove back to the hotel, Steve wondered if he had been a little harsh with the engineer, but then dismissed the notion. After all, he would need Jones's cooperation and access to his computer system eventually, so he may as well get the engineer working over the coming bank holiday to have everything ready for him by Tuesday. And, as a clincher, Steve thought the guy was a prick and felt little guilt in showing both him and Shade who was in the driving seat of this investigation.

He turned up the music system as Paint it Black, by the Rolling Stones blared into the coming evening. With the official investigation into the capabilities of the Skyforce machines and setup being taken care of, Steve could concentrate on finding his saboteur. And he felt certain that whoever it was would make an appearance at the All-England Helicopter Championships.

THE SHADES

Martyn Shade sipped from an ostentatious brandy glass, thin liquid that was far older than he was slipping down his neck like boiled honey. His study was warm, lit by an open log fire, but Martyn shivered a little in his plush dressing-gown. The dream had woken him again, the same dream that woke him whenever he was feeling anxious.

In the dream he is ten years old again, a junior at Neville Holt boarding school. It is sports day, when the five houses compete against each other in various events and the parents attend to watch their children run, throw or jump. Martyn has been selected to run in the hundred meter sprint, and he stands waiting, dressed in his white vest and black shorts, stretching, his face locked in focus and determination.

He spies his parents. His mother waves and his father offers a reassuring nod. Martyn ignores them both. He is determined to win first place, just as his brother Carl had in the previous event, and have the coveted red ribbon pinned to his shirt. Martyn does not realise when his younger brother Henry sidles up beside him. The younger participants have already run their events, and Henry Junior, chubby and slow, had performed with predictably underwhelming results.

'Hallo, Martyn,' says Henry.

'I can't talk now, Henry. They'll be calling us to start soon.'

'Are you nervous?'

'Nope.'

'You look nervous.'

'Bugger off, Henry.' Martyn sighs.

'Daddy says its not the winning or losing that matters, but the taking part.'

Martyn turns a withering look to his little brother. 'Daddy only says that to make you feel like less of a failure. Winning is everything. Daddy wins everything. Carl wins everything. I'm going to win.'

The sports master calls the runners to the starting line.

'Good luck, Martyn!' calls Henry.

'Fuck off, dick,' Martyn mumbles under his breath. He takes his place along side the other children. He has nothing but contempt for his competitors. Not one of them have put in the serious time and training that he has. They all thought that speed and power was something that was acquired with age, but Martyn knew better. He knew that even an undeveloped ten year old could hone his body with exercise. He would leave his class mates in the dust.

The starter pistol fires and Martyn explodes into movement, his legs pounding against the grass, his arms pumping like pistons. A confident grin slides across his face as he eats up the track in wicked time.

And then disaster strikes. The world seems to slow down to stare as his foot catches on a loose clod of earth, and he trips, skidding face first across the track. He looks up through a blur of tears as the feet of other children run on over the finish line. He sees his father, his hand resting on the shoulder of his older brother Carl, who looks down at him through a mask of indifference.

In the dream, young Martyn knows rage. Absolute and unsullied rage.

The fire in the study popped and flared suddenly. Martyn sipped from the glass again, the sharpness of the brandy drawing him back to the here and now. That fateful sports day had been a small failure, a minor humiliation in the grand scheme of things, but it still had power over his dreams. Even now, independently rich and successful, the suspicion that his father had favoured Carl over him filled him with a drive to compete against his brother. To compete and win.

The crushing of Helispech GB had been one of the sweetest moments of his life. He had celebrated the day that Carl had lost his final client. Alone, he had taken bottle of his most expensive champagne to the grave of his father. Once there he smashed the bottle over the tombstone and walked home, surprised at the enormous sense of loss that had overwhelmed him.

He knew then that power, riches and women would never bring him the true satisfaction he craved. It was only by beating Carl that he would feel complete. And tomorrow he would. The All England Helicopter Championships would see Skyforce piss all over Helispech, of that he was sure. More importantly, it would be Martyn Shade piloting and, sweetest of all, he would have Henry Junior as his navigator.

It had taken a lot to convince his younger brother to go against Carl in a public competition. Henry had always been content to muddle through life sitting on the fence, refusing to be drawn into open conflict, but after years of being in Carl's shadow, even someone as placid as Henry began to feel resentment.

Martyn gulped the last of his Brandy and made his way to bed. Tomorrow Carl would be defeated by his only family, and the world would know once and for all who was the favoured son. Not for the first time Martyn wished his father were alive. Just so he could see the look on his face.

He climbed into bed beside his wife, who mumbled something in her sleep and turned away. For a long time Martyn stared at the ceiling, sleep eluding him. His mind churned with excitement and anticipation for tomorrow's competition. It would do him no good to be unrested for the upcoming trials, he knew. He needed to be at his best.

He briefly thought of taking one of his wife's valium, and then decided against it. Such weakness, he felt, was unbecoming of a man of his stature. He then thought of getting dressed and paying a visit to Valerie, who had an almost artistic knack for putting him at his ease, but no, it was too late for that.

He let his mind wander, searching for more peaceful times in his life. A faint grin spread across his face as his thoughts settled on one of the sweeter moments in his life. One of his most elegant victories agains this elder brother, and one that only Martyn knew about. He smile widened as he thought back to day after his father's funeral- the day the family solicitor had announced the Henry Shade Senior's last will an testament.

*

Martyn fumed, standing on the veranda of the family home and smoking a cigarette- something he rarely did. A light drizzle spattered around him, and in the distance thunder rumbled.

Family home. The thought almost made him spit.

'Martyn?'

Martyn closed his eye at the sound of his brother's voice. Henry was being characteristically placid about the whole thing. 'What it is, Henry?'

'Why don't you come inside? It's raining.'

Martyn turned around. 'Is it, Henry? I honestly hadn't noticed.'

Henry smiled, the same worried smile he always gave when someone was drawing him into confrontation. 'It's not that bad, is it?' he said.

Martyn had to restrain himself from punching his younger brother there and then. 'He got the entire family business and the family home. I was bloody raised here and now it all belongs to him! Everything!'

'But the money, Martyn. We've more money than we could ever spend! And Carl says we're welcome to work over at English Steel.'

'Work for Carl?' Martyn's eyes narrowed. 'I really don't fucking think so, Henry, do you?'

'Well, I don't mind. It's a nice salary and all the perks.' Henry shrugged.

'That's not the point, though, is it? The point is we'll be working for Carl.'

'So don't work for him!' Henry said, laughing. 'Take the money and go live on a beach somewhere!'

'Oh, they'd love that, wouldn't they?' said Martyn. 'Martyn the man of leisure. Martyn the sponger.'

'Who?' said Henry, exasperated. 'Who'll say these things?'

For a while neither brother spoke.

'Look,' said Henry. 'You've got capital. You've got contacts. You can do anything you want. Anything. All this anger isn't getting you anywhere.'

Henry walked back into the house, leaving Martyn staring across the grounds. Martyn threw his dwindling cigarette to the ground and stubbed it out with his foot. A weak habit. One he would have to get rid of.

'Anything,' he mumbled. Henry, as much as he lacked backbone, was right. Martyn *could* go into business for himself. He'd need a lot more capital, though. A lot more.

Martyn's eyes became steely as he thought of a plan. Carl had gotten more than his fair share of father's belongings- not just the house, but a host of antiques, art works and furnishings. Even a valuable Krugerand collection. Martyn grinned. He could take the Krugerand, sell them, and have everything he needed to go into business. And best of all he could do it all at Carl's expense.

Security at the family estate was tight, with cameras at the walls and a manned guardhouse at the gate. He would need a way to take the collection without being caught, and a way to enter the grounds without being seen. Arriving by helicopter would be ideal, but for the noise of the rotors. Martyn smiled, remembering an old proverb his father had used to paraphrase- 'There are no problems in life, only opportunities.'

Bullshit, of course, but in this case pertinent.

That night Martyn put his plan into action. After calling in a few favours he had hired a different helicopter than the model he was used to- opting for a smaller two-seater Skyforce with floats instead of skids. Starting up the machine, he flew into the night, logging the co-ordinates of the family estate into his GPS. The night was pitch black with heavy cloud cover; ideal for what he had in mind. He rose to 12,000 feet, breaking through the cloud and into a brilliant star-speckled sky.

As the helicopter approached the GPS co-ordinates, Martyn took a deep, steadying breath. His heart was thudding in his chest. What he was about to attempt was something he had never tried before. The theory was solid, but the practice could prove to be fatal. As he reached his position, he cut the engine.

He had only seconds to gain control after the engine cut. He lowered the collective lever, gaining gliding control of the copter. He descended into the thick cloud, gravity snatching at his machine like a jealous toddler. The copter yawed violently, but Martyn's training and skill swiftly brought the machine back under control.

Martyn's eyes darted about the dashboard readouts, constantly checking his speed, rate of descent and that he remained straight and level. He had worked out in his flight plan that it would take exactly twelve minutes to break cloud cover, and after a heart-stopping additional thirty seconds, he broke free five-hundred feet above his former family home.

Scanning the grounds, he quickly spotted a ribbon

of water reflecting what little light there was and glided the machine carefully down until he was fifty feet above the river that ran through the estate. He then pulled back on the stick very, very gently. He would only get one shot a the landing, and it would have to be perfect. The helicopter touched down on the river with barely a splash. It was a dangerous way to land, but it was, above all, a *quiet* way to land.

Within seconds he had swam to shore and tethered the helicopter to a nearby tree.

Martyn crept through the grounds, his black wetsuit effectively camouflaging him in the dark night. Gaining entrance to the house was easy- the dogs knew his scent and Carl had rather foolishly left the key-codes for the backdoor unchanged.

Within minutes he was in his father's old study, recognising the smell of pipe-smoke and leather. He went to the huge safe in the far corner and tried the code. Again, nobody had yet thought to change the combination. He loaded up the Krugerands into a hold-all and carefully locked the safe behind him. Then he jogged quietly back out into the grounds, the excitement of the night air filling him with glee. It was all he could do to stop himself laughing in triumph.

He made his way back to his helicopter and cut the tethering rope. Then, using a long branch, he guided the machine along the banks, letting the river carry him quietly away from the grounds. He kept an eye on his GPS, and when he was exactly a mile from the house, he started the ignition. As he waited for the engine to reach its correct operating temperature, he felt the bag next to him. More than a million pounds worth of gold, and certainly more than enough to set up a nice little business.

But what business? On what grounds could he compete with his brother? The answer seemed obvious. Helicopters. Helispech was a dominant force in the world of British aviation, and a prestige feather in the cap of English Steel. Martyn was certain that, with his new injection of capital, he could wipe Helispech off the map.

When he was a safe enough distance from the Shade grounds, Martyn flew the helicopter back into the night sky.

The perfect crime, he thought.

*

The night before the All England Helicopter Championships, Martyn Shade slept like a baby. A small smile hung on his face as he dreamed of triumph, glory and the humiliation of his elder brother.

THE CHAMPIONSHIPS

The All-England Helicopter Championship was held every mayday bank holiday at Barton Hall in Lincolnshire. Steve had heard a lot about the Hall at the barbecue the previous day- namely that a finer example of eighteenth century architecture would not be found outside of London.

In his time he had been invited to a few stately homes, and always recommended the golden rule; the bigger the gravel drive the bigger the house. Barton seemed to be an exception to the rule, though, since Steve had drove his Lexus through the outer gates he had driven past an eighteen-hole golf course, a twenty acre lake, three outdoor tennis courts, a swimming pool and a helicopter pad. It was only at the final set of electronic security gates that he reached the hall, and found a surprisingly short and circular gravel driveway in front of the magnificent four-storey mansion.

There were only a few cars parked on the drive, Steve correctly assumed that many of the guests would be flying in. He stepped out of his car and craned his neck to take in the one hundred bedroom house, reflecting, not for the first time, that it might be nice to be obscenely rich. It was all a far cry from the two-up two-down he had grown up in.

Still, a hundred rooms seems a waste for a house, he thought, it would make a brilliant hotel and casino. Very James Bond.

He walked around the west wing of the house until he could hear the noise of helicopter engines. He was running late for the first day, and assumed the flying skills test was already underway. He was proved right as he rounded a corner to the rear of the building and saw a swarm of machines, some waiting to take off, some just landed, and some still in flight.

Unlike the recent Skyforce day at RAF Cottesbrooke where all the machines had been the same, Barton hosted a myriad of different models. The navy was in force with four Gazelles- a twin-engine turbine helicopter that was a large model compared to the Skyforce. There were also several Bell helicopters, and even a few Hughes helicopters. Steve also noticed the English Steel's executive 109, standing out from the nearer machines like a cheetah in a herd of gazelle. The assembled choppers made an impressive sight, and a large military twin-rotor Chipmunk helicopter completed the impression of a chopper anorak's dream come to life. Amongst the varied and colourful helicopters, the Skyforce Two plus Two model was also well represented.

Steve was moderately surprised by the number of spectators that had come to enjoy the day, but judging by the amount of attractions it seemed the day was just as much about having fun as watching the competition. There was a fairground for the kids, beer tents for the adults, and all the usual gaming and souvenir stalls. There was even a bungee jump tower for the brave at heart. Steve reflected that certain aspects of his security investigation were starting to feel more like a holiday than an assignment, and he found himself a shady place to stand as he watched the helicopters burr around like monstrous gilded bees, each busy preparing for the days challenge.

The principle of the flying skills test was quite basic. The pilot was in charge of flying the machine while his co-pilot held onto a rope, on the end of which was four-inch circular ring of steel. Attached to this ring by two ropes was a bucket containing two gallons of water. The exercise was straightforward; each helicopter had sixty seconds to take off, hover taxi at a height of about ten feet across to a horizontal pole, and hook the ring holding the bucket onto the pole. This had to be done within the minute, without one drop of water being spilled. Each team was given five attempts. After looking at the score board Steve saw that all of the navy teams had already taken their turn, and that out of all the competitors only one had scored maximum points. The task was obviously not as easy as it sounded.

There was a brief smattering of applause and Steve turned his attention back to the cordoned off competition area, where a Skyforce Two plus Two was currently prepping for its turn on the bucket run. On closer inspection, Steve realised the competitors were John and Doug. He watched with amused interest as John bought the chopper to a gentle hover and Doug leaned out of the passenger side ready to take up the slack on the bucket. Their first attempt was a no-hoper, with Doug failing to bring the bucket under sufficient control before the sixty seconds were up. More laughable still was their third attempt, when Doug managed to lose control of the bucket completely, tipping its contents to the ground. Knowing they had lost the round beyond redemption, Doug reeled up the bucket and put it over his head, rousing laughs and cheers from those on the ground who knew him. John titled the nose of the helicopter in a mock bow, before flying to the chopper park, landing and then, knowing John and Doug, most probably heading to the beer tent.

The next helicopter up was the Augusta 109, and Steve was surprised to see that Carl Shade himself was to be piloting on behalf of English Steel. He recognised the man from his files, but would have pegged him as Martyn's brother regardless. Though Carl was older, keeping his greying hair cropped close to the skin, he shared the same stance and aura of confidence as his brother. Steve's heart skipped a beat as he saw Carl's co-pilot approach. It was Marnie, dressed all in black as usual; with the same comfortable knee-high boots on as the last few times he had seen her. Steve tried to catch her eye to give her a wave, but she didn't even look in his direction, her mind seemed to be wholly occupied with the helicopter preparations.

It was easy to appreciate Carl Shade's piloting expertise, especially after John and Doug's comical attempts. The older Shade brother bought the big 109 to a flawless ten-foot hover while Marnie kept the bucket under complete control, hardly even wavering during the hover taxi, and slotting the metal ring home on the first attempt, well under the sixty second cut-off point. There was an appreciative round of applause from the crowd. Carl was obviously an accomplished flyer, but whether he could match the navy boys would remain to be seen. Sure enough all of the attempts went as smoothly as the first, bar the very last try when the bucket snagged on the pole, necessitating in a second attempt which, while successful, fell slightly outside of the allotted sixty seconds. Carl Shade has scored a respectable four out of five, placing him overall second in the competition so far.

Steve was relieved when the final Chopper engine shut down for the lunch break, giving his battered eardrums a well deserved rest. Lunch was a running buffet, and Steve was intending to seize the opportunity to casually question some of the guests that had been at Skyforce on the day of the attempt on Martyn Shade's life. At least that had been his intention. Instead he found himself inevitably drawn to Marnie.

'Well done,' he said.

Marnie turned around, and Steve was taken aback by the flashing aggression in her eyes.

'Well done, my arse. He cocked it up on the final try and had the nerve to blame me. I mean, you saw it, didn't you? The bucket was as steady as a rock, wasn't it? When we landed he gave me a right roasting, the arrogant bastard!'

Steve raised his hands in supplication. 'I assume you're talking about Carl Shade?'

'Too bloody right I am. The prick. What is it about men with power that make them such insufferable arseholes?'

'I wouldn't know,' said Steve, chuckling.

Marnie sighed, putting a delicate finger to her forehead. 'I'm sorry, I'm behaving like a total cow. How are you, Steve?'

'Doing fine, I suppose,' Steve smiled a sardonic half-smile. 'Fine for someone who's been so flagrantly used and abandoned.'

Marnie frowned, seeming to wonder what he was talking about before a light of recollection shone in her eye.

'Oh, of course. Sorry for running out on you, I did mean to call but…'

'It's okay, you don't have to explain yourself. We're all grown-ups here.' Said Steve. 'It's a shame,' he added, 'Rambleton do a brilliant breakfast.'

Marnie smiled, and seemed about to speak when they were interrupted. Carl Shade approached, wearing a Saville Row suit despite the clement weather.

'Marnie, I'm leaving,' he said. 'I'll be back tomorrow for the navigation course ready for take-off at nine sharp. Be ready.'

Steve used the opportunity to introduce himself. 'Carl Shade, isn't it? C.E.O of English Steel?'

Carl turned to him as if noticing him for the first time. 'That's right,' he said.

Steve held out his hand, which was shaken with little enthusiasm. 'I'm Steve Allen. I'm a friend of your brothers.'

Carl gave a phantom of a smile and nodded with the bare minimum of politeness before turning back to Marnie.

'Remember, Marnie, get to bed early and no alcohol.' And with that he marched off.

Marnie stared daggers at the back of the man's head as he walked away. 'Yes, Mr. Shade, no Mr. Shade, three fucking bags full Mr. Shade,' she muttered, before storming off without another word.

Steve was left standing on his own, surprised by Marnie's unprecedented temper. Obviously being a rude arsehole was in the Shade genes, but Marnie's reaction had been overly childish. He wondered briefly if such a potential for bad attitude was enough to put him off her, but supposed, regretfully, that it wouldn't be. He had a feeling that if she came calling he'd go running to her like a lap dog.

He was still smiling to himself when he turned back to the buffet table, and then the smile dissolved quickly, replaced instead by a death-mask of shock. He had noticed Rupert Cooksley standing by the table, apparently deep in conversation with a man. Steve might have dismissed this totally, assuming Rupert was with a boyfriend, but something about the man's face- a haunted glint to his eye, a plastic falseness to his smile- made him examine the companion more closely. Steve remembered his training and hid his shocked reaction, turning his involuntary step backwards into a casual turn. He walked away with convincing nonchalance, resisting the near maddening urge to turn around and look at the man again, to see if he had been spotted in return.

It was Michael McConnell.

Steve couldn't believe it, the last time he had seen the man he had sported a thick black beard and moustache and long black hair. He had been a pallbearer at the IRA funeral when Steve's deep cover operation had been blown to pieces. It had been

McConnell himself who had ordered the attempt on Steve's life that very night, sending his own fiancé and her brother to their unanticipated deaths.

But what was he doing here and now? Could he be involved with the attempt on Shade's life? Steve doubted it. McConnell had only just escaped at the time, and it seemed unlikely he would rush head long into a murder attempt… even if he was a total psychopath. Also, death by sabotage was a little subtle for McConnell's tastes, and what would he have against an upper-class English businessman, other than the fact that he was rich and English?

No. Though Steve was always quick to doubt coincidence, he didn't think McConnell was here for Shade. Which left the unsettling question; why was he here at all? And with Rupert Cooksley of all people?

It only left two options; either McConnell had finally come looking for him, or…

He made it back to his car without looking over his shoulder or quickening his pace, once there he picked up his cell phone and punched in the personal number of Niles Bailey.

'Niles here, is that you Allen?'

'Yes, sir, I have some urgent information.'

'Is your line secure?'

Steve cursed silently. 'No, sir, there really isn't time. I think you need to know this right away.'

There was a pause before Niles continued. 'Go on.'

'Its McConnell, sir, he's here, at the helicopter championships in Lincolnshire.'

'But that's impossible! Our last intel update had him placed at some training camp in Libya.'

'Your intel's wrong, sir. I saw him with my own

eyes. With the MP Rupert Cooksley, no less.'

Nile's bafflement was clear in his tones. 'Why the bloody hell would he be hanging around a helicopter championship with an English member of parliament?'

'It's obvious, sir. They're after the Royal.'

There was a long pause before Niles replied. 'You think the IRA is planning some attack against the prince? How does this fit in with the sabotage on Shade's helicopter?'

'It doesn't, sir, and I don't think that the IRA are necessarily behind this one.'

'You think McConnell is operating on his own?'

'It wouldn't be the first time, sir. You remember the Sandringham incident?'

Nile's laughed mirthlessly. 'Of course, who doesn't?'

Steve began scanning the estate grounds behind him in the wing mirror of his Lexus, suddenly feeling vulnerable in the open.

'Well, we know how much damage he's capable of.' He said. 'I advise we take him down now. I'll keep a tab on him until you can...'

Niles interrupted. 'You'll do no such thing, Steve. He knows your face, and if he clocks you, you may force his hand. There's still weeks before the Royal visit. I want this handled with utter discretion and an absolute minimum potential for collateral damage.'

Steve's eyes narrowed with annoyance. 'You mean you don't want the papers getting wind that a dangerous escaped terrorist is rubbing shoulders with England's finest?'

'I'll remind you that you are addressing a superior officer, Commander Allen.' Said Niles, his tone turning icy.

Steve gritted his teeth. 'I'm sorry, sir, but I above all know how dangerous McConnell can be. We can't let him go about unchecked.'

'He won't be unchecked. I'll be taking this information to M15 immediately.'

'With all due respect, sir, this is my security operation.'

'Commander Allen, your job was to assess the suitability of a training ground so that a VIP might indulge a hobby. You are not Special Air Service anymore, and this is not some bloody western! McConnell will be taken care of, but not by you.'

Steve remained silent, for a while. 'You're making a mistake,' he said, eventually.

'That's your opinion and my prerogative. In the mean time, collate what is left of your report and bring it back to me as soon as possible. I don't want you going back to the championships.'

'Yes, sir,' said Steve, defeated. He hung up the phone and for a time merely stood, staring into nothing. Then he got into his Lexus and made his way back to Rambleton Hall.

On the drive home he set the cruise control to 50mph while he battled with an emotional cocktail of shock, disappointment and anger. He tried desperately to focus on the job he had been assigned to, but his thoughts kept returning to the time, long ago, when he had come up against McConnell with the chance to kill him- and had blew it.

THE SANDRINGHAM INCIDENT

Steve had only been involved with the Royal family directly once before. After his third tour of Northern Ireland, and now with the rank of captain, he had successfully completed his sixteen weeks of training at Hereford and was now a full member of the SAS. It wouldn't be long until he returned to Belfast, though this time out of uniform and under cover. In the mean time he had been temporarily assigned to the Royal Protection Unit.

He had felt enormous pride when he had first learned of the assignment, and had privately fantasised about walking boldly in front of the Royals wherever they went, like the American Presidential bodyguards; cool and vigilant against any would-be assassin. As usual, the reality of the assignment was very different from Steve's private daydreams. His term of duty coincided with the Queen's visit to Sandringham in Norfolk, and it was Steve's job, along with a fellow SAS officer, to be responsible for the Queen's security for only one hour a day; when she walked her corgis along the beach after lunch. This occasional walk necessitated a constantly manned observation post built in the tallest tree in the area, where the on-duty SAS officer would base himself and spend his hours meticulously searching the wooded area that separated the private beach from the castle grounds. Nothing was allowed in our out of the area while the daily walk was in progress, and the Queen was not to be approached or hailed under any circumstances other than in the event of a direct security risk.

In short, the job was boring, uncomfortable and thankless- factors that seemed to be a constantly recurring theme in Steve's army career to date.

The shifts were twenty-four hours on and twenty-four hours off. Steve didn't know what was worse; a full day and night living out of a tree house or a full day and night back at his bed and breakfast in the nearby coastal town of Hunstanton, which in the off-season may as well have been a ghost town.

To liven up his long periods of hanging around with nothing to do, Steve had bought himself a BMW 1000cc motorbike, and liked nothing more than to take a burn up and down the mostly deserted coastal roads on his days off. For the last few days though, sheets of rain and slick roads had made even that one pleasure an impossibility. But today was different; today the sun was making an unprecedented early autumn appearance, and Steve faced the pleasant prospect of spending his day off walking along the beaches in warm sunshine.

He thought of his fellow SAS man, Danny, who was on duty that day. It looked like he might actually get to watch over the Queen on her walk, the lucky git. The previous bad weather had kept her majesty in doors, meaning that Danny and Steve had had nothing more to watch over but a rainy and miserable seafront. Today's sudden change in weather would surely bring the Queen out for her constitutional.

Steve had decided to leave his bike at the bed and breakfast that day and, saying goodbye to his landlady, had taken a leisurely stroll into town, buying a bag of chips and enjoying the feel of the sun on his skin. He took a seat on a grassy area on the promenade overlooking the peer, where he could watch the fishing boats and generally laze the day away.

This is the life, he thought as he popped another hot chip into his mouth, enjoying the sharp bite of the extra salt and vinegar.

He wasn't sure what it was about the figure that made him so suddenly uncomfortable. Certainly with the change in weather there were a few new faces on the promenade, so Steve never knew exactly what made him focus on this one particular man. One moment he had been minding his own business, the next a figure to his right had caught his attention. He couldn't see what the man was doing, he just appeared to be looking out to sea, leaning casually on a white Ford Cortina parked at the side of the road. He was dressed in a long jacket, which seemed unusual considering the weather. But the thing that really caught Steve's attention was the stranger's bright red hair. He watched as the man smoked a cigarette with his right hand, and seemed to be scratching his back with his left.

Steve turned his attention back to his chips,

dismissing his uncomfortable suspicions as a soldier's paranoia. Then something made him look again. The red-haired man was now in his Cortina, fiddling with the ignition. The car faltered a few times and then started, the stranger driving off along the main road out of town. Steve shook his head, still wondering how such an unremarkable man in an unremarkable car could raise his hackles so. He continued eating, and idly reflected that the Queen would be beginning her walk around about now.

It was some minutes before a middle-aged man came walking up from the beach, a confused expression on his face.

'Where the bloody hell's my car?' He said to the world at large.

Steve stiffened, the chip in his mouth suddenly turning to tasteless mush. He stood bolt upright and began the sprint back to the bed and breakfast.

Soldier's paranoia. The thought seemed to mock him now. The red haired man had been no ordinary car thief; of that he was certain. A thousand alarm bells were ringing in his brain, and both his training and his instincts were telling him to get back to his post in Sandringham.

It was a three-mile run back to his digs, and it took every ounce of Steve's stamina to get him there at a full sprint. He briefly thought of trying to hail a taxi, but finding a taxi in Hunstanton would likely take him longer than running. He felt his first stitch come and go, and was seeing stars by the time he reached the Bed and Breakfast. He pushed past his startled land lady, grabbed his bike keys and within seconds was speeding down the road, his front wheel leaving the ground as he fought hard against the bike's awesome acceleration.

He was thankful of his knowledge of the roads as he drove the bike flat-out, twice nearly losing control on sharp bends, and once coming within centimetres of an oncoming skoda, briefly glimpsing the terrified face of the elderly driver.

As he neared the castle grounds, two anxieties circled around his mind. One, he hoped that he was wrong. Two, he hoped that if he was right then he wasn't too late. A white Ford Cortina abandoned by the roadside shattered any flicker of hope that he might be wrong about what was happening…

Steve had a brief moral dilemma of whether he should drive to the castle and alert the rest of the staff, or make his way directly to his post. He opted for the latter. Pushing the bike to its limits, he cut off at a concealed clearing that was the quickest way to the observation post. The way was thick with trees, impossible in a car and insanity on a bike, but Steve didn't let up on the throttle, risking almost certain collision to shave precious seconds off of his arrival time.

As he approached the tree house, he slowed the bike down only sufficiently to jump off, letting the BMW roll into a tree with a crunch. He called out for Danny but there was no reply. Suddenly he spotted the crumpled form of his companion in a nearby bush. Danny was dead. Clearly dead. A knife hilt was protruding from his throat and a slick of blood covered his light armour vest. More ominous still, his rifle was missing.

Steve felt a swelling tide of panic in his belly. The

Queen was going to be shot with one of her own soldier's rifles.

With a quickness born of sheer adrenaline, Steve scaled the rope ladder to the observation platform above. He thanked his lucky stars as he saw that his kit was still stowed safely away, and his own rifle lay untouched. He briefly debated going to lower ground to see if Danny's killer was still nearby, but opted instead to make use of the high vantage point and the rifles powerful telescopic sight.

He adjusted the sight on his M16A1 and scanned the beach. It didn't take him long to locate the Queen, walking in blissful unawareness with three of her dogs. Steve's brain whirred with possibilities as he tried to remember all of the possible sniper points he and Danny had come up with in various boredom-born thought exercises. The M16A1 they had been issued with had state-of-the-art sighting, so distance wouldn't be a problem even for someone with only rudimentary firearms training. Steve scanned the underground between himself and the beach, desperately tracking for any sign of the assassin. He was convinced the sniper would fire from cover rather than risking an open shot, but there was just so much cover to hide in!

In later days Steve would reflect that the attack would have been completely successful if not for one thing- the attacker's bright red hair. As he scanned through the greys and greens of the undergrowth, the bright patch of red drew his attention as sure as any flare. There was the sniper, a cigarette clamped calmly between his lips, gazing coolly through the sight of his stolen rifle. With clarity born of experience and training, Steve fought through his panic and steadied the cross hairs on that patch of red. He squeezed the trigger gently for a single shot.

Bang! Bang!

Two shots? Steve looked up from his sight and realised that not only had the patch of red hair disappeared from sight, but that the Queen had fallen to the ground. Had he been too late?

Shit!

He practically fell out of the tree while he fiddled with the two-way radio, shouting for assistance. He hit the ground running, and made his way over to the patch of ground where the sniper had lain, heedless of his own safety. When he got there he saw the stolen M16A1 laying discarded on the ground. A sticky patch of blood on the ground told Steve his shot had rang true, wounding, but apparently not disabling his target. He once again had a flash decision to make; should he attempt to pursue the attacker, or should he male certain the Queen's safety? He chided himself for even thinking there was a choice before running off in the Queen's direction. As he ran he screamed once more into his radio.

'*Where's my fucking backup?*'

He burst out of the undergrowth and onto the beach, seeing the Queen hunched over in the distance. She turned her head as she heard him approach.

Thank God, thought Steve, *she's alive.*

As he got closer he realised with relief that the Queen appeared uninjured, and also saw that she was weeping.

'Ma'am?' he said, hesitantly.

The Queen didn't reply, only waved a hand to signify that she was unhurt. Steve kept a respectful distance, keeping his rifle close at hand as he scanned the undergrowth, hopefully shielding the Queen with his own body from any possible line of attack. As he stood, two corgis sniffed curiously at his boots.

The tight knot of tension in his gut didn't lessen until he heard the army Gazelle helicopter come round to land nearby. He took the Queen's arm to help her on board and only then realised what she had been huddled over. A bloodied corgi. Dead. Shot clean through the head.

THE TELEPHONE CALL

Steve lay in his hotel room, staring blankly at the ceiling. A smoked-salmon sandwich sat on the dressing table by his side, untouched, and his Mac Powerbook sat open and neglected, its eldritch blue glow the only light source in the room.

His eyes were dark and distant as the events of the past week circled around his head. He tried to work up the motivation to further compile his report, but couldn't. He was angry, and even as he lay down he could feel the tension of adrenaline tightening his muscles.

He had phoned Valerie under the pretence of asking how the rest of the competition went, but really to see if she had noticed anything out of the usual. Maddeningly, she didn't mention anything about Rupert Cooksley and his new 'partner', but did reveal that Martyn Shade and his brother Henry had secured third place over all in the competition so far, having only just been beaten by two military trained teams. He had almost asked how Marnie and Carl had faired, but then, remembering that either sister had yet to mention the other, thought it prudent to keep quiet.

Steve got up out of bed in one swift movement and moved to the bedroom window, staring out over the moonlit Rutland Water. He clenched a fist and pounded it half-heartedly on the windowsill. To think that McConnell was not only free, but sniffing about on his patch. Had the ex-terrorist known that Steve was investigating Skyforce? Could he have been in someway involved in the sabotage on Martyn Shade's helicopter? Had the attempted assassination been aimed at him, rather than the Skyforce MD? It was easy to get lost in paranoia, particularly as he had done so much to harm Michael McConnell, and particularly as the man was such a notorious psychopath.

Never give an Irishman cause for revenge, thought Steve, mirthlessly, *Especially if said Irishman is as mad as a rabid dog.*

Thinking about it, there was some comfort in assuming that McConnell had come for him personally. That the man might have come to settle a grudge was straightforward and understandable, something that Steve could deal with. However, if there was some intricate plot involving the Real IRA, Skyforce and the Royal, then there could be more snakes in the grass than even MI5 could be ready for. Having seen his fair share of carnage in the course of his career, Steve would go to great lengths to avoid a sabotage attempt. The last thing he wanted was another Lockerbie.

Something else had been bothering him, although it had been a quiet, nagging concern at he back of his mind. He had a bad feeling about Richard Jones. One thing he had learned with his involvement in the world of aviation was that the key positions in an airline's flying schools and so on, were usually held by people who's integrity was above question. Jones's over-the-top reaction to Steve's knowledge of the Australian incident had been unusual. Did the man have something to hide? And if so, did he want it hidden badly enough to make an attempt on the life of a CAA officer? True the man had been posted in America during the time, but...

...Perhaps it was vanity to assume that anyone wanted him dead at all. After all, Martyn Shade had plenty of people who would benefit from his death. His wife and mistress had personal motives. His brothers had financial motive. Even Marnie had a motive- after all the man had been indirectly responsible for the death of her father and directly so for the ruination of her family business. But were any of them capable of murder?

He would interview Jones on Tuesday, but so far his report was going to draw one definite conclusion- with a mysterious saboteur and a possible Real IRA connection, Bromsfield was no fit place for the Prince to even visit, let alone learn to fly a helicopter.

He was interrupted from his thoughts by the sudden ringing of his mobile phone. He answered.

'Hello?'

For a while there was no answer, just the faint distortion of hot breath.

'Steve?' he recognised the voice. It was Val again... or Marnie? She continued speaking before he could find out.

'I meant to say... I missed you today. I didn't realise

you were going to leave so early. I was hoping we could meet up for a drink.' Marnie then. Her voice was slurred, as though she was slightly drunk.

'Yeah, sorry about that. I had to catch up on some work. Besides, you didn't seem in the mood for company.'

'Oh, I'm in the mood for company, Steve. I'm all dressed up for it. Or, dressed down, I should say.'

Steve smiled a puzzled half-smile while he wondered what to say to that. The voice continued.

'Just a pair of stockings, a basque and some stiletto heel shoes. Nothing else, just the basics. I'm just lying here, with a bottle of champagne, all by myself.'

Steve's tension was suddenly forgotten. 'That's a bloody shame,' he said. 'I'm sure we can do something about that.'

'Well, seeing as you're not around, I may as well get started without you.'

Steve's jaw hung open in shock as soft moans and dark rustlings began to sound over the phone. He'd seen phone sex lines advertised on the television, but he didn't realise that they could phone you.

He listened as the warm hurried sounds over the phone began to intensify.

'Oh god, oh god, Steve. I'm coming. Coming. Come and get me!'

There was a brief scream of ecstasy before the line went dead. Steve was dressed and had his car keys in hand before he even knew what he was doing, but he stopped abruptly. Marnie hadn't left him her address. He quickly looked up the number that had phoned him, and noted with dismay that it was a private listing.

He sat down on the bed with a sigh and an

uncomfortable lump in his jeans. He wondered if his luck could get any worse.

DAY TWO

The second day of the All England helicopter championships was by far the most difficult of the competition. It was generally a quieter day, and less entertaining for the spectators, as the nature of the navigation trials made following the action impossible. Throughout the day the helicopters would depart at timed intervals and fly a difficult low-level navigational course, a course only revealed to the pilots when a sealed envelope containing the computer print out of their individual flights was handed to them. Still, the steadily clement bank holiday weather was enough to draw back a big crowd, and the beer tents and gaming areas, not to mention the bungee tower, were all buzzing with activity.

The conditions of the navigation challenge were tough but fair. Each team set off at ten-minute intervals to a six point navigation course. Volunteers from the Helicopter Club of Europe were strategically at all way points to time the arrivals and to make sure that the pilots hovered their machines over the targets to prove they had found their way by good judgment rather than luck. The team that completed the course in the quickest time would be the winner. The Army and Navy teams had the advantage of quicker copters, but the private owners in their smaller helicopters held a distinct advantage in manoeuvrability, so the competition looked to be a close run.

Not that this was any concern of David Crisp. Davey was an MI5 agent, and had been since the tender age of twenty-three. Now, in his thirties, he still retained his boyish features. In fact, they were part of his strongest asset as an agent, and that asset was his ability to totally blend in almost anywhere he went. Whether it was an inner-city crack house or an elite members-only country club, Crisp had no problem seeming as if he totally belonged there. His easygoing charm, good looks and ability to mimic almost any regional accent had nearly lead him to pursue a career as an actor, but an early love of espionage drama like Mission Impossible and The Saint had led him to apply for MI5. Once there, he had quickly discovered that working for military intelligence was really nothing like it was on television, but he had excelled regardless, and quickly made a name for himself in undercover operations. Which was why he was in Barton Hall today, spearheading a joint operation with local police to box McConnell as discreetly as possible until an arrest could be made with minimal danger to the public.

He was in communication with five other field agents, one acting as a barman, two acting as litter pickers and two more under the guise of a married couple come to see the show. They were all in turn in communication with a surveillance team holed up in the top floors of the hall, scanning the grounds from their vantage point.

Crisp allowed himself a small smile. Basically, McConnell was fucked. He couldn't move anywhere without being seen, and even now local police were patrolling every access road to the area. However, it didn't pay to get cocky, Davey knew. He had read up on McConnell, in fact, the terrorist was something of a legend around his department, and as a new recruit he had been taken through several of McConnell's exploits as part of his training. The Irish man was good. Very good. But Davey Crisp was determined to prove he was better.

He sat in the breakfast tent, only a few seats down from where McConnell dined with Rupert Cooksley. Crisp had dressed in casual summer wear, expensive and trendy, his brown hair was kept floppy and devil-may care and he left just a smattering of stubble on his pointed chin. His near-transparent aviator-style sunglasses, discreet gold chain, and expensive shop tan completed the image of a man born into money, and someone who went to these kind of events for the prestige and the networking. He pulled the look off well, and his final touch, a solid Lincolnshire accent cross-bred with a bit of universal yuppy, was just enough to make him blend into the money crowd with ease. Better still, the aura of business-rat on leisure-time gave him an excuse to be almost constantly on his mobile phone, which was fitted with a transmitter linked directly to the rest of his team.

Currently he was chatting away about rugby to an

indifferent businessman from Hull. He was being just obnoxious enough to be convincingly genuine, and so far had warranted no suspicious glances from McConnell's way. This was good; he had ingratiated himself into the crowd with minimal fuss, meaning he could stick to the terrorist's position with ease.

There was only one upset in the breakfast tent that morning. The Shade brothers, Martyn and Henry Junior, had started arguing. From what he had overheard, Davey learned that Henry had been out drinking the night before and was suffering the worst of a hangover, and as such he was unfit to navigate. Martyn had promptly reported Henry as officially too sick to compete, meaning he was within his rights to draft in a new navigator. Henry had looked miserable, but relieved, and the argument had ended as quickly as it had begun. Davey couldn't help thinking that the younger Shade brother looked like a painting of a sad clown, with his curly black hair and comically glum expression, but he refrained from staring too hard; he had a cover to maintain after all.

When the PA system announced the pilots to prepare for the start of the competition, Davey followed the crowd out casually, as if he had known them for years, still chatting with the Hull businessman as though he had struck up a genuine rapport- other than simply pestering a man too polite to tell him to fuck off. He kept a comfortable distance from McConnell and watched with satisfaction as the two agents posing as a couple moved casually to a box-in position.

McConnell was flying with Cooksley today, and if all went to plan they'd both be apprehended by armed response as soon as they landed, conveniently clear of any civilians while they waited for the rotors to spin down. It would be a clean take, and if the shit did hit the fan there were patrol cars ready on every road out of the area. Crisp had made sure they pulled out all the stops on this one and he could afford no embarrassment. He was looking forward to finding out just what the hell Michael McConnell thought he was doing rubbing shoulders with England's great and good.

*

Robert Cooksley went through his pre-flight checks on his helicopter once again. He had spent breakfast studying the computer printout of the navigation test with its six timed stages. Unlike the last year the route wasn't a simple wide circuit, but one that required he double back to certain points. This had struck him as unnecessarily dangerous, as he'd have to be constantly alert to the risk of running into his fellow competitors. Nether-the-less he had memorised the route until he knew it like the back of his hand. And frankly, he had been grateful for the distraction…

McConnell had been hiding in Cooksley's barn now for what seemed like an age, reducing Rupert to the role of manservant in his own home. He had had to smuggle food, drink and entertainment to the Irishman, all the while hiding the fact from his wife and son. The stress had taken a physical toll on the normally pristine MP. His hair seemed greyer, his eyes were deeply hooded and his face drawn tightly. And all the while he had had to smile his politician's smile, hoping that no one would guess that Rupert Cooksley's newfound best friend was a former IRA psychopath.

He felt a tap on his knee and looked over at McConnell's face, which was split by his familiar broad and sardonic grin.

'Not too much longer, my English fancy man,' he said, with a chuckle. 'It wont be too long 'til all these wankers think I'm your husband or something.'

Rupert, despite his inner fear and rage, had to agree with McConnell. The man seemed to have a knack for ingratiating himself with people. He had only accompanied Cooksley to a few Skyforce social events and already the big Irishman was more popular than he was. It made him sick to his stomach, especially when he thought about why Michael McConnell was so eager to be accepted by the Skyforce crowd.

'Chin up, boyo,' said McConnell. 'You keep smiling and before you know it I'll be out of your life for good and you can go back to not shagging your wife.'

Rupert Cooksley grabbed the cyclic control lever hard enough to turn his knuckles white. They were to be the second to take off for the navigation course, and he couldn't wait. Anything to take his mind off the demon beside him.

*

John James prepared for take off, taking one last look at the flight plan.

He shouted through is head set to his co-pilot Doug. 'I don't like the feel of this one, Dougie. It's not like last year when we just had to fly in a big circle. We've got to cut back on ourselves. Like at the Battle of Naseby monument. We're supposed to be hovering over that at two minutes past ten on the dot. We've really got to be on the ball today.'

Doug laughed. 'If you were that worried about being on the ball, you wouldn't have had us up drinking all night with Henry Shade.'

John joined in with his friend's laughter. 'Did you see him this morning? I thought he was going to throw up in his breakfast!'

'Well, I guess he doesn't have our powers of recuperation, John-boy. And also…' Doug reached into his pocket and pulled out a small electronic device. 'I bet he didn't smuggle in a personal GPS system. I logged in all the waypoint co-ordinates this morning. We can't go wrong!'

John put on a mock scowl. 'That's against the rules, Dougie. Maps and compasses only.'

'I know, John, but I want to win,' said Doug.

'Well, I suppose that's alright then.'

The two were still laughing as their helicopter began its ascent.

*

David Crisp watched as Rupert Cooksley's helicopter took off, and kept watching until it disappeared out of sight. He doubted McConnell had spotted any of his crew, but he had stationed plain clothes officers to act as spotters at each of the waypoints just incase the helicopter took any unexpected detours. His lips were dry in anticipation. This would be the biggest collar of his career.

*

Ten minutes after Rupert Cooksley departed, the English Steel Augusta piloted by Carl Shade and navigated by Marnie Johnson took off. And soon after him, Martyn Shade took off in his Skyforce Two plus Two, a new navigator replacing his hungover younger brother.

Henry Shade watched as the helicopters became specks on the horizon. He still felt guilty about letting Martyn down. He had been looking forward to the two of them knocking Carl off his high horse in a rare display of family unity, but now that didn't look like it was going to happen.

Still, the day wouldn't be a total waste. Not while there was a beer tent to be explored.

*

That morning had found Steve staring at the ceiling of his hotel room. He had slept little during the night, adrenalin pumping unbidden through his veins, and the face of Michael McConnell flashing into existence every time he had closed his eyes. The ache of knowing the Irishman was out there, not a few miles away, and that he could do nothing about it filled him with irritation.

He sat up suddenly, determination setting his jaw. He might not be allowed to attend the second day of the helicopter championships, but he refused to waste the bank holiday moping. Besides, with the bulk of Skyforce's employees attending the championships, he had the perfect opportunity to have a nose around Bromsfield Airfield.

After a quick shower he was in the Lexus and eating up the miles of country road with no delays. When he arrived there, he was surprised to see that the airfield wasn't as deserted as he first thought it would be. Although the Skyforce building looked empty, the airfield itself was still busy, with the local flying school's students practicing touch and go landings in the circuit.

Steve parked his car in the flying school car-park and walked the few hundred yards to the Skyforce building. As he expected the door were locked and alarmed. He briefly thought back to his younger days when breaking and entering would have involved some breaking, but he had more sophisticated means at his disposal these days. He took the electronic scrambler from his pockets and punched in the code he had obtained from the security company that had designed the system. Within seconds he could hear the electronic doors within the building deactivate finishing with the two main sliding doors in front smoothly opening before him. Steve grinned. Crowbars and jimmies had their place, but you couldn't beat a bit of good, clean technology.

He walked through the hangar and made his way to the stairs that led to the office block. Once again he marvelled at the cleanliness of the workplace and the beauty of the helicopters in various stages of being serviced. Some had their main rotor blades off, some were minus their tail rotors, and there were several lying on the benches awaiting testing. Steve felt a little guilty about his suspicions concerning Richard Jones. It was obvious he ran an immaculate operation.

Steve spent a careful few minutes inspecting the

flight briefing rooms, but found nothing of interest. He saw a door with the sign 'MD Secretary' above it, and went into what he assumed was Val Johnson's office. He looked around briefly before sitting at her desk and noting the conference telephone system. He stared at it with bemused interest for a while,on the digital list of recently dialled numbers, his own contact number was still quite prominent. A funny idea was forming in his head. Was it Val who had phoned him last night? It seemed a long way to go from Barton Hall just to make a dirty phone-call at the office. He shook his head and concentrated on the matter at hand. He took the phone and pressed the button marked 'Richard Jones', and hearing a ringing on the other side of the hanger, it wasn't long before he was in Richard's office.

Gaining access to Richard's IBM had been easy; once again utilising a piece of customised hardware that, as much as he didn't understand how it worked, had made a nonsense of Richard's basic security encryptions. Steve note that he'd have to send a thank you card to the boys in tech before the week was out.

He took a piece of paper out of his pocket in which he had hastily scribbled the registration of the Skyforce Two plus Two that had disintegrated mid-air in Australia. He opened up the model database and punched in Golf Britain Five Five Whiskey and the details came up on the screen instantly. Steve frowned at the information. The serial number of 0010 meant this was an early production, and would have been well near its limit of two thousand flying hours when it had been sold on to the private customer in Australia. In fact it had been sold on with nineteen hundred hours on its clock. According to the technical logs it had only flown for forty seven hours once under new ownership- meaning that the chopper still should have had fifty-three hours of flight time remaining before needing a major overhaul.

All of this information went against what Jones had said at the barbecue. The chief engineer had stated that the chopper was well out of hours before the accident. Why lie? To save face?

Steve copied the database onto a memory drive and left the office as he had found it. Outside in his Lexus he ran the engine, and in the cool air conditioning, tried to think things through.

The service record for the Australian machine had clearly stated that it had been serviced at regular intervals with tits annual inspection had been current. It had been sold on with a three year Certificate of Airworthiness. But Richard had been adamant the machine was out of hours when sold, a statement totally contradicted by the records. Were the records incorrect, or had the machine been faulty?

Steve sat and stared for a while at his dashboard. His own mileage was approaching the time for the twenty-thousand-miles service. He tapped his steering wheel thoughtfully. If he were so inclined it'd be the work of a day to have his mileage clocked back to ten thousand, and so saving him the expense of a service. Could the same be done for helicopters? And if so, why would that benefit Skyforce?

He looked over at the Helispech building and noticed the hanger doors were open. No sense sitting here wondering, thought Steve, and made his way over to the hanger.

Once there, he noticed once again what a far cry the Helispech hanger was from the neat and ordered Skyforce operation. Parts lay scattered haphazardly, patches of sawdust covered oil stains at random intervals, and a radio blared loud dance music ceaselessly. He heard a clanging from the direction of the an old Hughes 500c.

'Hello?' he shouted.

There was another clang and the radio stopped abruptly. A huge figure emerged from the shadows, a grubby shaved head erupting from heavily oiled overalls. Steve noticed a spanner the size of his forearm in the giant man's fist.

'What is it?' said the man with a gruff Scottish accent.

'Hi,' Steve smiled brightly, reasoning that this the wisest thing to do when a man twice your size is glaring at you suspiciously. 'I was talking to Marnie Johnson the other day about buying a helicopter. I had a few more technical questions, but if she's not here I'll just go.'

The big Scotsman's face split with a crooked grin. 'Yer in luck,' he said. 'I'm just going on lunch. The name's Archie. Anything you need to know about a chopper, I'm your man. At least that's what it says on the toilet walls, whut?'

*

Later at a greasy spoon cafe, Steve watched with interest as Archie polished off a fried breakfast that probably would have given a bear a heart attack. Archie chewed on the last of his bacon and gestured his fork at Steve's plate, raising his eyebrows inquisitively. Steve smiled and pushed the rest of his half-eaten breakfast over to the big man, who began eating it with little pause.

'You see, Archie,' he said. 'I'm interested in buying a second-hand machine, but these things aren't like a ford cortina, am I right? If I get a faulty helicopter I can't exactly pull it over to the roadside and call the AA?'

Archie chuckled and carried on tucking in to the rest of Steve's breakfast.

Steve continued. 'So I suppose what I really want to know is- what guarantee have I got that the flight hours on a second-hand machine are the same as the hours stated in the log books?'

'Easy-peasy,' said Archie, still chewing industriously. 'Every helicopter has a DATCOM similar to a mil-o-meter in a car that automatically starts recording the hours as soon as the engine is started up. So, you know, no bother.'

'That's fine,' said Steve. 'But surely they can be altered to show a lower reading? Like clocking a car?'

Archie stopped chewing and swallowed, fixing Steve with a serious glare. 'Except its not like a car is it? These engineers are responsible for people's lives. It's like you said- there's no hard-shoulder at five hundred feet. Besides- weren't you on about buying a Skyforce Two plus Two?'

'Yes, I was.' Steve said.

'Then there's no way their DATCOM can be altered. It's not manual, it's all electronically controlled by the main flight computer. All very advanced.' Archie said.

The two men shook hands with smiles when they

left the cafe, but inside Steve was furious. Another piece of a puzzle that led nowhere. For a while he had entertained the possibility that somebody was simply trying to make a few extra quid by clocking second hand helicopters, but if Archie was right, then the level of expertise needed to hack a flight computer seemed far and above the skill set of the average thief making a few quid for himself here and there. Anybody with that kind of computer expertise would be a high earner, and unlikely to endanger lives for the sake of a such meagre and infrequent rewards.

Steve had barely returned to his car when his mobile phone began ringing. He accessed the screen and froze as he saw the text message that had appeared. Only two words. Code Red. The last time he had seen such a general alert had been when the IRA had bombed Oxford Street at Christmas.

THE CATASTROPHE

Louise Sharp was enjoying the sun. She had only really volunteered to help with the Helicopter Club of Europe to fill up an otherwise empty weekend. After spending the entirety of her Sunday endlessly patrolling the danger areas with the other safety marshals, ensuring the stupid and the curious didn't get too close to the helicopter rotor blades, she had quickly reconsidered her decision. She had been hard pressed to think of a more boring afternoon. Thats why when she had received the phone call that morning telling her she had been upgraded to navigator's waypoint observer she had been quietly delighted. No public, no high-visibility jacket, and the only helicopters she would see would be comfortably far off.

She had jumped into her brand new MGF sports car that she had received for her eighteenth birthday two weeks prior, had picked up her boyfriend, Mac, and had driven out to her posting- The Battle of Naseby Monument.

It had taken a while to find the monument, which was situated in a field seemingly in the middle of nowhere, but once there they set up two deck-chairs, left the radio running on the car and sat back in the perfect bank holiday weather.

'Don't forget these,' said Mac, handing her a stopwatch and the list of the competing helicopters, their crews and their ETAs.

'Oh, sod them,' said Louise. 'If I see another helicopter today it'll be too soon.'

'Well we didn't come all the way out here to catch a tan did we?' said Mac. Louise grinned brightly, and John shook his head. 'One of these days we must have a talk about your work ethic,' he said.

'Listening to the music won't run the battery down, will it?' said Louise, suddenly.

'Not for a long while,' said Mac. 'Why?'

Louise lay back in her deck chair. 'The chap on the phone said I was to flash the headlights three times to signal that the helicopters are in the right place.'

'You'll have plenty of battery left for your headlights. And besides-' Mac grinned mischievously. '- if you do run out of battery you could just flash something else, couldn't you?'

Louise landed a playful cuff alongside Mac's head, ruffling his wavy hair.

The young couple waited a while. 'What time is it?' Said Louise snapping awake from a quiet doze.

'Relax, it's only about nine-fifty,' said Mac, checking his expensive watch.

Louise frowned. 'Well have we missed any? They were supposed to be here for nine-thirty.'

Mac shook his head. 'Clear skies all morning. I'm not surprised. Look how long it took us to find the bloody place- and its not as if they can just pull over at the nearest Little Chef and ask directions, is it?'

Louise chuckled at the thought, and then cocked her head. 'Hang on,' she said. 'I think I hear something.' She stood up ad surveyed the skies and saw all four helicopters converging on the monument from four different directions.

'Well at least one of them's got it right,' Mac said.

Louise looked at her stopwatch and carefully noted the time of 10.04 a.m. Then she turned, her pretty young face creasing with concern. 'This doesn't seem right,' she said.

'Well, what did they tell you to expect?' Mac asked.

'Nothing, really. Just to mark down the arrivals. Nothing like this.'

Mac bought a mobile phone out of his pocket. 'I'm going to call someone,' he said, now shouting over the noise of helicopter engines. 'Who did you speak to this morning?'

Louise shook her head. 'He didn't say. I didn't think to ask his name...' She turned around, searching the skies, and then her jaw fell in horror.

Above the rumble of the helicopter engines another sound was beginning. Another, much louder, sound. It was the unmistakable roar of high-speed fast-approaching low-level jet fighters.

*

David Crisp was worried. He knew from experience that it didn't take long for a nagging doubt to become a full-on fuckup. And he had a nagging doubt. He tried to remain in cover as he chatted into the transponder in his mobile phone, but he was finding it increasingly difficult to keep his cool.

He cursed his earlier confidence. 'Pride Comes Before A fall' had been words his mother had lived by, and like most of his mother's words, Davey had usually just ignored them. Now he was beginning to see the wisdom of the phrase as he sensed the beginning of something dreadful that he couldn't quite put his finger on.

'What do you mean "no sighting"?' he barked into the phone.

Collins- one of the men he had stationed at the way points, keeping an eye on the helicopters- sounded baffled. 'I haven't seen a single chopper, man. Was there a delay at your end?'

Davey shook his head. 'I'm getting the same line from every waypoint- nobody's seen a chopper in fucking ages. They should have been sighted by now. What the fuck is going on?'

'I've asked around with the officials,' said Collins. 'None of them know what's going on. They're as in the dark as we are.'

'Not fucking good enough!' shouted Crisp, drawing a few startled glances from the crowd around him. 'Four helicopters do not just disappear!' Davey lowered his voice. 'Especially when there's an at-large murderer on board one of them!'

'What do you want me to do?' Said Collins.

'Just wait.' Replied Crisp. 'I'm going to get on the blower to the RAF. They've got radar. I'm going to get them to track every single chopper and tell me what the fuck is going on.'

'You could get them to radio the pilots, tell them to land their crafts and hold their positions until we get there?' replied Collins.

Davey thought for a while. 'Maybe,' he said. 'I'll find out where they are first. There's still a chance this could just be a mix up. Let's not blow our loads just yet, ay?'

'Copy.'

*

The last of the four helicopters to arrive at the scene was Two plus Two piloted by John James and navigated by Doug Williams.

'What's going on?' shouted John. 'There's supposed to be a ten-minute separation time.'

'Just bring us in to hover,' replied Doug. 'Keep us well away from the other guys.'

This was a strategy echoed by Carl Shade, who along with his co-pilot Marnie opted to break into a low orbit away from the scene of congestion. And by Rupert Cooksley and his co-pilot, who, inadvisably, tried to fly backwards away from the monument.

Martyn Shade made no such efforts to avoid his competitors. As far as he was concerned he had arrived at the designated co-ordinates first, and damned if he was going to give up on victory just because of somebody else's cock-up. He and his young co-pilot hovered smugly near the Naseby monument, awaiting the attention of the ground spotter. It would be the last victory Martyn Shade would ever know.

*

Davey's ground his teeth as he was put on hold getting through to at RAF Cottesbrooke. 'Do these people not understand the meaning of the word "priority"?' he mumbled to himself.

He checked his watch as he had done a dozen times already. He couldn't quite place it, but he had a feeling that something was about to go terribly wrong.

*

The morning training flight for the two German Tornadoes had gone very well, and Ober-Lieutenant Franz Smith had slowed the formation down to about two hundred mph in preparation for their last turning point before joining the long finals for RAF Cotterstock and, although he was flying quite low at two hundred and fifty feet, he considered himself to have good all-round visibility with no problems for a routine landing.

With a mixture of white-faced horror and trained professionalism he instantly reacted as he spotted the helicopters. At the last second a burst of power sent the Tornado climbing high, skimming over the prone helicopters, and only just avoiding them.

Unfortunately, perhaps because the second Tornado was flying directly behind and only slightly to the left of the other pilot, it was too late reacting and flew straight into the helicopter of Martyn Shade. The young co-pilot died instantly, the Tornado's wing decapitating him at baffling speeds. A scream came from Martyn Shade as his body was pulverised by force and impact, torn from its seat and hurtled two hundred and fifty feet to the ground below. The helicopter itself was sent spinning crazily downward, its fuel tank not yet ruptured, but the body itself a twisted cartoon of its previous form.

The Tornado had lost its left wing, but fuel was stilled being pumped into its jet engine, sending the craft plummeting downward. The pilot lost precious seconds as he tried to wrestle control of the doomed craft. The navigator, however, instantly hit the red button that fired the jet rockets that powered the ejector seat. He shot wildly into the air and parachuted to safety. By the time the pilot had realised that all was lost and hit his own ejector button, the Tornado had already smashed into the side of a small wooden copse. With an earth shaking explosion, debris and shrapnel was sent pelting into the countryside.

The shockwave from the explosion was the final straw for the already off-kilter Helicopter of Rupert Cooksley. He gritted his teeth as he tried to gain some control from the descending chopper.

'You fucking slag!' roared McConnell. 'Fly the fucking thing or we're going to die!'

'Then at least we'll both burn in hell you stinking, ginger, psychotic bastard!' roared Cooksley. The helicopter made a hard landing it was never designed to withstand. The machine tilted over, its rotor blades smashing everything around it, churning up clods of earth before shattering into lethal pieces. McConnell was flung unconscious from the cockpit. Rupert Cooksley was not so lucky. He died in the mangled wreck instantly, his face and lungs impaled on a shaft of grey metal.

John James' Skyforce machine was hit by the same blast shockwaves as Cooksley, but was able to lessen the impact by diving away at speed. Running purely on instinct and adrenaline, he put the helicopter down in a successful landing in a field near a red sports car. He and Doug emerged shaking and wide eyed.

'What the hell happened?' murmured Doug.

'Are you okay?' said John, he grabbed Doug's shoulder, as if to attest he was still there. Then he looked over to the young couple b the sports car, who were standing in dumbfounded horror. 'Is everyone okay?' Called John, his voice cracking with shock.

Louise turned to him and opened her mouth as if to reply. And then she screamed, and screamed, and did not stop screaming until she fainted.

Mac pointed a shaking finger to the wreckage of Rupert Cooksley's copter. 'That man, moved!' he said. 'He's alive!' The young man began running toward the wreckage.

'Stay here with the girl!' ordered John. 'That thing's leaking fuel!'

Mac hesitated a while, his body caught between two courses of action. Finally he settled on standing with his hands to his head as he watched John race over to the stricken man.

Doug shouted after him. 'What the hell are you doing, man! Get back here, the fuel's leaking!'

John didn't reply, just sprinted over to the unconscious man and hoisted him into a fireman's lift. He began to run back, unsteady under the weight of the stranger. Doug hesitated a moment and then ran over to help his friend. As he ran he noticed that a small fire had started in the helicopter wreck.

'Get down, its going to blow!' he screamed, jumping onto John and bringing the three of them down to the ground. They felt the earth pound beneath them as the fuel ignited and a fireball ripped into the sky. Then they were on there feet again, hauling the stranger between them in a chairlift. They reached the car and put the body down carefully.

Doug grinned. 'All in all,' he said. 'That could have been a lot worse.'

John said nothing, just shook his head and pointed down at the ground. Mac's body lay sprawled on the grass. He hadn't ducked when the explosion happened, and a piece of shrapnel from the engine block had punched through his chest, ending his life almost instantly.

Doug sat on the ground, dizzy with horror and adrenalin. Neither he nor John noticed as the stranger they had rescued regained his senses and made his way over to the car. They did not even notice when the car started and drove into the distance.

*

Carl Shade and Marnie had landed the Augusta helicopter as close to Martyn's wreckage as they could. As they exited the chopper, Marnie caught sight of the german navigator, limping along on a leg soaked with blood.

'You go and see to him,' said Carl. 'I'll see what I can do for Martyn.'

Marnie nodded and jogged toward the navigator while Carl made his way over to his brother's body. He walked past the wreck of the helicopter. There was nothing to be done for the pilot. It would take a skilled crew a long time to pry his remains from the wreckage.

He wasted no further time rubber-necking at the

scene of horror, and began walking to his brother's body again. To his immense surprise, Martyn Shade was still alive. It was obvious that every bone in his body had been smashed to a pulp. What had once been a man was now a ruin of twisted muscle and flesh. Martyn would die, no question, but for now he pulled in ragged breaths and fought to focus his one remaining eye on his brother. Carl looked down at him through a mask of indifference, and somewhere in his broken mind Martyn began to feel rage.

'Oh, Martyn,' said Carl. 'You always had to take things so fucking personally, didn't you?'

*

David Crisp arrived at the Naseby Monument at the same time as Collins and two other team members. He took in the scene of destruction before him with horrified awe.

'Jesus,' muttered Collins. 'How the fuck is this allowed to happen?'

'Worry about that later,' said Crisp. 'I want the survivors interviewed and I want McConnell found-now!'

The team split up. Davey walked over to the nearest survivors. A grey haired man cradling a hysterical teenage girl, and a portly man putting a jacket over the bloodied body of a younger man.

Crisp flashed his ID badge. 'I need to know the whereabouts of Rupert Cooksley's co-pilot. Did he survive?'

Nobody answered.

'I need answers now, dammit!' roared Crisp.

The young girl put her hand over her ears and sobbed louder still. The man cradling her gave Crisp a fierce look.

'Please!' Said Crisp. 'The man is dangerous!'

The portly man turned around. 'He survived,' he said. 'We pulled him from the crash site.'

Crisp's heart began beating wildly. 'Where is he?' he demanded.

The man shook his head. 'I don't know. But there was a red sports car here and its gone now.'

'What kind of car?'

The man shook his head again, a hopeless look in his eye. 'A convertible? I don't know the model...Jesus. Jesus did you see the blood?'

David Crisp turned from the man, sensing he'd get nothing else useful any time soon. He once again shouted into his mobile phone. 'Time to get the locals involved, people. I want this area locked down. Michael McConnell is on the loose and is thought to be driving a red convertible. I want every road blocked immediately. And remember- this man is extremely dangerous.'

Davey put his phone in his pocket and turned to survey the smouldering wreck of the helicopter and the distant plume of smoke where the Tornado had crashed. He gritted his teeth in frustration. The weight of human tragedy here was terrible- but to top it all off, one of the most dangerous men in Europe had been able to use the accident as a smokescreen to cover his escape.

'Fuck,' he said. He couldn't think of anything to add to that. 'Fuck.'

CODE RED

Steve gunned the Lexus, barreling around the twists and turns of the country road, mobile phone pressed tightly against his ear. Eventually the ringing stopped and a female voice answered.

'Hello?' It was Tracy, Nile's secretary.

'Tracy is that you? Where's Niles, I've been trying to get through for ages.'

'You and everybody else. I'll patch you through.'

There was a brief click and then Niles Bailey was on the phone. 'Steve, we have reports of a major aircraft incident. A Tornado from Dusseldorf has had a midair collision with one, possibly two, helicopters from the championships at Barton Hall.'

A cold shiver ran down Steve's spine. 'How many dead?' he asked. *Marnie*, he thought, *Don't let it be Marnie.*

'Five reported dead. Emergency services are on the scene and the areas clamped down. The local forces are running with MI5 boys, so they're locking things down.'

'Where did this happen?'

'Battle of Naseby monument, one of the many navigation waypoints used by the Tornado squadron.' Niles replied.

'And you say there was more than one helicopter involved?'

'Apparently there were four at the scene; two landed safely. Two didn't. The two that didn't belonged to Martyn Shade and Rupert Cooksley.'

Despite the awful news, Steve found himself breathing a sigh of relief. Marnie, at least, had avoided catastrophe. 'Any survivors?' he asked.

'Shade, Cooksley and a young co-pilot by the name of Summers are all dead. Apparently Cooksley's co-pilot survived.'

Steve slammed on his brakes and pulled into a lay-by. 'McConnell was with Cooksley.'

'Yes.'

'Tell me we've got him.'

Niles was silent for a while, and then let loose a heavy sigh. 'He managed to escape the crash site before anybody could get there. But we have the area locked down!'

Steve bit his lip. 'We should have got him when I first spotted him.'

'God damn it, Steve. Nobody could have seen this coming.'

Steve closed his eyes. 'What can I do to help?'

'With McConnell? Nothing. Everybody on the ground is looking for him. David Crisp is heading the crew, there's no way he'll be able to stay out of sight for long.'

He's done it before, thought Steve.

'What I want from you is some answers, Steve,' Niles continued. 'I want to know how it is possible that four helicopters wound up in the same place at the same time. Secondly, find out from RAF Cottersbrook what the hell two Tornados were doing in an area that had temporarily restricted airspace. I've heard of some cockup's in my time, Steve, but this takes the biscuit.'

'Do you suspect sabotage?' Steve said.

'Yes.' Replied Niles. 'Crisp and his team have already had to blow their cover- that leaves just you to keep your ear to the ground. Get to Barton Hall, mingle with the pilots, find me some answers, Commander Allen.'

The line went dead and Steve stared hard ahead of him. Then he dialled the number for RAF Cottersbrook. 'Flight Lieutenant Griffiths, please,' he said, when he finally got through to air traffic control.

The voice that answered was heavy with fatigue. 'Griffiths here, how can I help?'

'My name is Steve Allen, I'm phoning-'

'Is this about the Naseby monument?' Griffiths interrupted.

'Yes,' said Steve, taken aback.

'Look, I can only tell you what I've told everybody else literally a hundred times today. Yes, there monument is often used as a visual reporting point by all the pilots, depending on which runway we are using at any given time. And, yes, we had notification several months ago from the Helicopter Club of Europe about the navigation course they had been allowed to select this year, and, no, the Battle of

Naseby monument most certainly wasn't on that list. If it had been then there's no way any Tornados, British or European, would have flown anywhere near it.'

Steve thanked the Lieutenant for his time, hung up, and began the drive to Barton Hall. As he drove he tried to think through how many pilots were with him that day at Cottesbrooke, and had listened to the flight controller give the exact time and place of the positions of low-level high-speed fighter planes. And, of the pilots who were there, how many of them would have been able to alter the navigation courses of the contestants?

As Steve pulled into Barton Hall he realised he was dealing with a devious maniac. And that didn't include McConnell- there was no way the Irishman could have derived nay benefit from the horrific smashup, especially seeing as he had nearly been killed himself.

He had to find out the true motive behind this madness if he was to have any chance of finding the killer. All he knew for sure was that of the couple of dozen people he was going to try and talk too that afternoon, several would have been at the air traffic control lecture and one of them was a cold-blooded killer. A killer who not only had opportunity to access flight control computers, but also had the knowledge to access them.

It was strangely quiet when he got out of his car at Barton House. There were still several helicopters in he parking area, but there was no noise of any flying activity. The fairground was silent, and the beer tents were being dismantled. But it was the crowd of people gathered at the bungee tower that gave Steve a cold feeling in his gut.

He made his way through, politely pushing past the gawkers. The site that awaited him was horrific. It was Henry Shade, or at least the body of Henry Shade, spread across the grass in a smear of blood. His legs were missing.

'What happened?' said Steve.

'A terrible accident,' murmured an old lady close by. She was standing, as were the rest of the crowd, as though transfixed by the gruesome scene and unable to leave. 'The ambulance is on its way.' She put a handkerchief to her lips and balked slightly.

Steve looked up at the dangling rope of the bungee tower. Henry Shade's legs still hung from it like a grotesque halloween decoration. It didn't take long to realise that this had been no accident. Somebody had tied the rope preceding the elastic section of the cord to the rope that followed it. When Henry Shade had jumped- and Steve couldn't think what would have possessed him to jump in the first place- he had fell suspended by a bungee chord with no elastic give in it. As he had reached the bottom of his descent, instead of the stomach-churning bounce as he rocketed back upwards, he would have only felt the brief terror as the knot tightened, and perhaps lived long enough to hear the sound of muscle and bone being ripped apart from the rest of his body.

Steve felt sick to his stomach. This was another premeditated murder. Committed by somebody who, undoubtably, must have ingratiated themselves utterly into the world of helicopters.

Why had Henry Shade been killed? It seemed obvious- he had been killed because he hadn't been in the helicopter with Martyn Shade when it was obliterated by a Tornado. He was supposed to have died with his brother, but hadn't flew because of his hangover. Had he been drunk when the killer enticed him to the top of the tower? Most likely, but then the killer would still have to have been somebody that Henry was familiar with.

Steve made his way back through the crowd and walked past the magnificent gardens to the restricted area behind the hall where most of the pilots were gathered in the flight planning marquee. The atmosphere was very subdued, and it was obvious to Steve why the helicopters were still stationary.One by one the pilots, navigators and competition personnel were being questioned by two uniformed policemen, trying to put together the last known whereabouts of Henry Shade in the hours leading up to the incident. A few people had placed him at the beer tent, curing his hangover with a bit of hair-of-the-dog, but nobody had placed him anywhere near the bungee tower.

After a couple of hours chitchatting with the pilots, and learning very little more than he already knew, Steve made his way to the Lexus and drove back to Rambleton Hall for an early night. He had deliberately avoided talking to Richard Jones. He was looking forward to cornering the man at his leisure, especially now that he had hard evidence he wanted to confront him with.

As he drove Steve thought about the Tornado pilot, and Rupert Cooksley, and the young co-pilot Summers. To have their lives snuffed out so suddenly and violently. All of them caught up in somebody else's game. A game intended for Martyn and Henry Shade. And what of Carl? He had narrowly avoided death at the Naseby Monument. Would the same killer who did for Henry come to find Carl?

That was a worry that could wait. Carl would be under police protection for the time being, and with Crisp and his team combing the streets for McConnell, any killer with sense would be lying low.

Tomorrow he would have answers. Would Skyforce UK still have a future without Martyn at the helm? Would Richard Jones be able to explain away the damning evidence agains his safety procedures? It could all wait for tomorrow, when the still fresh horror of the day had dulled a little.

As Steve drove up the long gravel drive to Rambelton Hall, he noticed the reflection of blue flashing lights in the distance. At first he thought there might be a fire, but as he rounded the corner he could see it was a police car.

What now? he thought.

He stopped his car and got out to see what the problem was. Two policeman turned to him. The larger of the two spoke. 'Mr. Allen?' he said.

Steve frowned, puzzled at how the policeman knew his name. 'Yes?'

'I'm arresting you for the murder of one Henry Shade Junior. Anything you say-'

Steve laughed. 'There's been a mistake, lads. Let me explain...'

'Resisting arrest are we?' Said the large copper. 'We'll soon see about that!' The big man grabbed Steve by the scruff of his jacket, without thinking the ex-SAS man's instincts kicked in, and he swatted the policeman's hand away. Realising what he had done, Steve then put his hands up. 'Look, seriously, just let me explain-'

He didn't see the truncheon until it was bearing down on him, and so was only able to deflect the blow partially. It was still enough to put him down. As he lay on the floor and the stars wheeled above him he tried to make sense of what had just occurred. He couldn't believe what was happening, but he was damned if he was going to sit back and let it happen. When the smaller policeman bent down to handcuff him, Steve kicked him in the balls, sprung to his feet and head-butted the larger man, who dropped to the ground as if poleaxed. The smaller policeman had now recovered and jumped onto Steve's back. Steve retorted with a vicious elbow to the ribs, then grabbed the man's hair, twisted out of the hold, forced his head back and punched him hard in the throat. As the smaller man lay choking, Steve had little time to congratulate himself. Four more policemen had turned up.

Deciding it would be more sensible to surrender, Steve put his hands in the air, once more hoping to explain. It didn't do him much good. They all kicked the shit out of him anyway.

The last thing he remembered was being trussed up like chicken with steel wire cutting into his wrists and ankles, and them using his head as a battering ram ad they tried to put him in the back of the patrol car.

There was a sarcastic voice saying, 'Well, fuck me, I've forgot to open the door.' And that was the last thing he remembered before waking up hours later on a wooden bench in a concrete jail cell.

THE SUMMARY

The clang of the cell door being thrown open against the stone wall was enough to raise Steve from his truncheon-induced slumber.

'You've got a visitor, arsehole,' roared an unfamiliar voice.

Steve slowly felt the back of his head and gingerly gauged the size of the lump that sprouted there like a malignant golfball.

'I can safely say this is one of the worst days I've ever had,' he grumbled.

'Judging by the way you look, I'm inclined to agree.' This time the voice was familiar.

With great effort, Steve opened his eyes, and then waited until the face before him swam into focus. Then he frowned. 'What the hell are you doing here?' he said.

'What the hell am I doing here?' Said Niles, eyebrows raising. 'I could ask you the same bloody question.'

'I got bored with the Rambleton,' said Steve. 'I thought I'd try some something a little more rustic.' His sarcasm lost some of its effect when, in a sudden wave of dizziness and nausea, he threw up on the floor.

Niles turned to the policeman at the cell door who was watching Steve with disinterest. 'You have five minutes to get this man a doctor, me some breakfast, and fetch me a policeman with a brain that can explain to me why a high ranking member of the MOD can be held in an English jail cell without his superiors being notified.' Niles's voice was calm, but the undertone of menace was apparent enough. The policeman's smirk dropped quickly from his face, and he hurried out into corridor.

Niles turned back to Steve, who was still lying flat on the bench, hands over his eyes. 'Commander Allen,' he said, 'you really are a magnet for bad news.'

*

An hour later they were sat in the police canteen, Steve putting his third icepack on the back of his head, Niles polishing off the remains of his double egg yolk and toast.

'So, then,' said Niles. 'Sum it up for me, Commander. Separate the shit from the fan for me.'

Steve grinned. 'It's mostly shit if I'm honest.'

'Try anyway.'

Steve looked up at the ceiling, marshalling his thoughts. 'You sent me to investigate Skyforce. That turned out to be a damn sight more difficult than first expected. We've had an unsuccessful attempt on Martyn Shade's life, we've had falsified safety records, we've had a successful attempt on Martyn Shade's life. What's more somebody even went to the trouble of murdering Martyn's brother, Henry.' Steve sighed. 'And lets not forget that Carl Shade was at the murder scene of Martyn- he could have just as easily been killed.'

'So somebody's got it in for the Shade brothers?' said Niles.

'It would seem so,' Steve replied. 'And me by proxy. Someone tipped the police off onto me, and it had to be somebody who knew my cover. What puzzles me is why anybody wants the Shade brothers dead so badly. I can't think of a strong enough reason- other than the fact that they were all insufferable pricks.'

Niles gave a short bark of laughter. 'If that were grounds for murder there'd be nobody left to kill.'

'So other than a motive, we still need a suspect. McConnell would seem the most likely candidate-'

'Well, he is a known killer.'

'Yes, and he'd be straight at the top of my list but for two things; one, he was nearly killed at the Naseby incident, and two, somebody's gone to great lengths to make the murders look like accidents. That's not McConnell's style. If he was going to target a prominent English family he'd want everybody to know exactly how and why he murdered them. The fucker'd probably leave us a business card.'

'So who are we left with?'

Steve thought for a while. 'Who's capable of engineering fatal accidents and badly wants the Shade brothers dead? I honestly couldn't say. Industrial espionage would seem the safest bet. After all, if

Skyforce are cleared for a Royal patron, the boost to their reputation will take them head and shoulders above their closest rivals.'

Niles sighed. 'That's not what I wanted to hear, Commander. I need solid suspects. I've got the PM breathing down my neck on this. The whole world wants answers and they expect me to give them. Worse still, with McConnell still out there I can't risk you hanging around here for very long.'

Steve looked up sharply. 'Why not?'

'You killed the man's fiancee, Steve,' said Niles. 'If he sees you he'll kill you. You may force his hand before we're ready for him. I can't risk it. We need him back behind bars, or we all look like a bunch of idiots.'

'Politics?'

Niles nodded. 'Politics. I want you out of this area as soon as possible.'

Steve nodded. 'I've got one more lead to follow up; Richard Jones, the chief engineer. I know he's been tampering with records, what I don't know is why. I've got some pieces of the puzzle here, Niles. I just need time to put them together.'

Niles drummed his fingers on the table for a while.

'I've got an appointment with him at nine o' clock this morning. At least let me interview him. If he's been falsifying service records like I suspect then he's directly responsible for the death of an Australian citizen. If I can get that over him, he might be willing to tell me just what the fuck is going on at Skyforce.'

Niles sat back and looked at his wristwatch. 'Well, its seven-thirty now. Crisp and his team are still trying to block McConnell. I can hold off the PM for about twelve hours before I start having to make our findings public. As soon as that happens, all bets are off. When McConnell realises we're on to him, he'll go to ground. And whoever's behind the murder attempts will likely do the same. If you can get me some hard names before this evening, there'll be a bloody OBE in it for you.'

Steve laughed. 'Let's get out of here then,' he said. 'Drop me back at Rambelton Hall and I'll take it from there.'

*

The first thing Steve did when he got back to Rambleton was take a shower. An evening at Her Majesty's Pleasure hadn't done much for his aroma, and a nice, hot shower stream was just the thing for when you'd had the crap beaten out of you. As he carefully washed his hair, trying to avoid the nasty lump on his head, he made the sensible vow that he would never hit a policeman again.

The Lexus coupe performed beautifully as it covered the thirty miles to Bromsfield airfield in thirty minutes flat. Steve was early for his nine o' clock appointment, and noted that Jones's car was already parked in the slot reserved for the Chief Engineer. He parked up next to it and approached the building. He was surprised to see that the front doors were still locked shut. He banged a few times and rang the buzzer, but nobody came to let him in.

After a while, Steve checked around the back of the building to see if there was any activity in the hanger. Once again, everything was locked shut. So where was Richard Jones?

He looked out over the active runway, where the local flying school had started early with one Cessna waiting to take off while another, obviously a low hours student, was bouncing his way down the runway attempting to land. It was then that Steve spotted the Skyforce Two plus Two model in the far corner of the airfield. Its blades were turning, and Steve could faintly hear the sound of the engine idling. He was too far away to see inside the tinted windows...

He paused, realising what was wrong with the picture. Helicopters didn't have anything that would restrict their all-round vision. No Skyforce chopper in the world would have tinted windows. The cabin was filled with smoke.

Steve started to run at full speed across the active runway, causing the pilot of the Cessna to swerve wildly as he tried to take off. Steve pointed frantically at the distant helicopter and made signs, with his hand to his ear, for the astonished flyer to radio the tower for help

As Steve approached the helicopter he ducked down to avoid the spinning blades and took a handkerchief from his pocket, covering his nose and mouth to protect himself from the smoke that poured from the cockpit when he opened the door. He stepped back as the door opened, wary of any flames that might have been provoked by the sudden rush of air. As the smoke cleared a little he was shocked to see Richard Jones slumped in the far side of the cockpit.

Steve nearly made the fatal mistake of running around the back of the helicopter, where the rear rotor blades would have reduce him to red mist. He remembered himself and went round the front. As he went to open the door and check on Richard, he noticed that the large aluminium tube that drew the outside air into the fresh air vent of the cockpit had been disconnected and reattached to the stainless steel exhaust pipe. There was no fire. The cockpit had been filled with its own exhaust fumes. He opened the door to be greeted by a vacant stare of a man who had been dead for some time. More gruesome still was the envelope gritted in his teeth. Steve gingerly took the paper from the dead man's mouth and began reading Richard Jone's suicide note.

I'm sorry, it read, *I killed Henry Shade Junior last night...*

Before Steve could finish reading the note, the body of Richard Jones, as though annoyed at being disturbed, slumped slightly in its seat. Its hand- which was still holding the copters cyclic control in a vice-like grip- slipped. Steve had just enough time to dive clear of the spinning rotor blades before the whole machine reared up like a wild stallion, the rear rotors smashing into the ground with an ear-splitting crash.

Steve sprinted away from the helicopter as fast as he could, but he still felt the force of the explosion as first one of the main rotor blades struck the ground, quickly followed by the parts of the the rear rotor rupturing the fuel tank. One hundred litres of aviation fuel blew the whole wreckage fifty feet into the air. As the machine flew for the last time, the body of the already dead pilot ground, only to be covered seconds later by mangled molten metal that cremated him almost instantly.

Steve hadn't seen any of the helicopter's last moments. He was lying face down and praying he wouldn't be hit by any of the shrapnel. He raised his head when he heard the sound of a fast approaching fire truck. He stood up as the truck screeched to a halt beside him, and notice with some surprise that it was Archie, the big Scots mechanic, that was driving.

The jovial man's face was set in unfamiliar seriousness. 'You all right?' he said.

'I'm okay.'

'There's an ambulance on the way if you need it.' Archie said.

'No, I'm fine,' said Steve. 'You stay at the scene, I'll phone the police.'

Steve walked swiftly away from the carnage. He had no intention of phoning the police, but he needed space to think. The accident had been no suicide, of that he was sure. He'd dealt with enough dead bodies in his time to know that the burst blood vessel in Richard's eyes had little to do with asphyxiation by smoke. Now that Richard's body was so much charred meat, it might be difficult for a casual examination to prove murder as a cause of death, but Steve doubted the flimsy pretence would stand up to real forensic examination.

The police would draw their own conclusions, right or wrong. Steve would concentrate on finding his own answers. Henry's death and now Richard's had both been hastily made to look like accidents. Somebody was getting desperate.

THE COMPUTER

Steve went back to his car and sat thinking for a while. The after effects of his run-in with the police coupled with the shock of the helicopter explosion had left him feeling drained and a little confused. With such brutal murders taking place, his thoughts would return to McConnell, but he knew that the IRA man had no experience of flying helicopters. Oh, he had co-piloted for Cooksley- but there was a world of difference between sitting in a passenger seat with a map and actually understanding how to fly one. And besides, all the attempts at subtlety were definitely not part of McConnell's MO.

Whoever had murdered the chief engineer of Skyforce had to have had a working knowledge of how to fly a helicopter, that much was clear. He suspected that Richard Jones had been dead before he was placed in the pilot's seat, and that the engine had been started and allowed to tick over, which would turn the rotor blades, but not to the extent where the machine would want to take off. Whoever set up the scene would have had to have wedgedRichard's dead fingers around the cyclic control, holding it steady enough to keep the rotor blades from tilting and smashing into the ground.

Steve looked out at the scene of the crash. The active runway had been closed and the mangled remains of the Skyforce Two plus Two were surrounded by emergency vehicles. The crash site was covered in foam and the fire crew were sifting through the wreckage for clues into the cause of the crash. It wouldn't take long for the accident investigators to find the remains of the altered air vent pipe and draw their own conclusions. If they thought that a suicide was the most obvious cause of the accident, would Richard's body even make it into more than a cursory forensic examination? He couldn't worry about that now...

With the workers from both of the helicopter companies gathered round to stare at the accident scene, Steve thought it would be an ideal time to have a nose around the Helispech set-up without anybody looking over his shoulder. He knew that Archie was still on duty, so if anybody challenged him he would simply come clean about his role in the CAA, and claim he wanted to interview Archie as a witness to Richard Jone's spectacular faux suicide. With only a few hours until Niles's deadline, Steve couldn't afford to waste time with cover stories anymore.

It wasn't long before he found himself in the Helispech hanger again. He looked up at the frayed rope where Alan Johnson had killed himself, his head removed from his body just as the rope had snapped.

Another suicide. Though, on a day like today, it was easy to imagine another murder, another conspiracy.

He walked through the deserted hanger, past the old Vietnam war Hughes helicopter, and that was when he saw a doorway he hadn't noticed before. Looking around to see if anybody was watching, Steve walked over and opened the door to look inside. There was another hangar, smaller and newer- an extension built and mostly hidden by the bulk of the main hanger.Right in the middle of the floor stood an immaculate English Steel Augusta 109 Power.

Steve walked over and opened the cockpit door of the 109, and the instrument panel lit up automatically like something out of a Star Trek movie. Slowly, Steve eased his way into the pilot seat. An electronic voice reminded him to fasten his seat belt, he ignored it and booted up the 109's onboard computer. The Augusta model was state of the art- far and above the economical Skyforce models. The computer offered the expected air conditioning controls and the global positioning satellite linked autopilot, it also automatically called up all the current UK and European weather readouts, plus a stormscope that would track and warn you of imminent thunderstorms.

He moved the cursor on to the main menu, accessing the flight plans submenu, and then punched in the date of the bank holiday collision. The display confirmed that the computer navigation plan for that day did in fact have the visual reporting point over the battle of Naseby monument at the third way point for exactly 10.04 a.m. With a little further investigation, the computer also offered an update on the weather, then ongoing navigation points, fuel and weight balance calculations and NOTAMS. Nothing incriminating, nothing even interesting.

Steve sighed and moved the cursor down the list of air notices, which included the notification of the All-England Championship, their whereabouts and duration, and also notification of a purple corridor in effect that day to correspond with a Royal flying out to Brighton. The very last item was the one Steve had been hoping for- information on military low-flying manoeuvres. He scrolled down the options available until he got to the European section. He then typed in Germany, followed by the aircraft type- Tornado.

A slow grin crept over Steve's face as the readout scrolled before him. The last visual reference point for the German Tornado's before finals that day was the Battle of Naseby monument- and whoever was piloting this helicopter had been fully aware of it. The pilot had been fully aware of the impending collision, and yet had flown there anyway, keeping well out of harms way, and at the same time also gaining the perfect alibi. The pilot had been Carl Shade, chairman of English Steel.

'Got you, you bastard!' Steve hissed.

'You're not talking about me are you, Mr. Allen?'

Steve blanched and turned around to look firstly into the face of Carl Shade, and secondly into the barrel of a Beretta 50mm pistol.

'Shit,' he said.

THE SOLUTION

'Mr. Allen,' said Carl Shade. 'Would you kindly get the fuck out of my helicopter? I have no problem shooting you, but I'd rather not get your brains all over the leather seats.'

'Very sensible,' said Steve, putting his hands up and exiting the chopper. 'It's not something you can really leave to the maid, I suppose.'

Carl indicated him to walk ahead of him, and prodded him with the Beretta occasionally as he was guided through another doorway and into what turned out to be a very large computer room.

'Sit down, Mr. Allen. Make yourself comfortable.' Said Carl.

Steve did so, staring around at the dozens of monitors and the myriad of information they displayed, from complex looking finance software to twenty-four hour news channels. There were displays from all around the globe, and facts and figures sprawled in a way that seemed incomprehensible to

Steve.

'I must confess, not many people get to see the nerve centre of my operation. you should feel lucky.' Carl grinned. 'When you deal with steel on a global basis it pays to keep connected. From here I can keep an eye on the whole damn world; stock markets, material developments, politics. All of it shaping the money markets, allowing me to buy the cheapest and sell the dearest. All of it painting the bigger picture,' he tapped his finger against his temple. 'The bigger picture, Mr. Allen, that's where I live.'

Steve nodded. 'And what part of the bigger picture was killing your brothers?'

Carl Shade's grin froze on his face, but the eyes behind it turned solemn. 'I was nineteen when my father died,' he said. 'I was training to be a concert pianist but then, because I was the eldest, I was suddenly chairman of the board at English Steel, responsible for twenty thousand jobs.' Carl looked directly into Steve's eyes. 'I had no choice. No choice at all. I had to live, breath and shit English Steel, and all the while my two useless brothers just pissed about, spending their money and whinging about how hard-done-by they were.'

Steve tried to maintain Carl's gaze, but in his peripheral vision he was keeping a close watch on the gun that was trained on him, waiting for the slightest slip that might signal an opportunity for escape. 'That was all years ago,' Said Steve. 'Why now? What's happened to change things?'

'Skyforce,' Shade replied. 'My whole family has always flown helicopters and, with all his spare time, that nasty little ingrate Martyn became an expert pilot.

When he extended his interest and set up a company to trade in helicopters, I just assumed it would be a passing fad. Nobody could have predicted it would become a worldwide success. Nobody would predict that Martyn would become a millionaire in his own right.'

Steve shook his head. 'Jealousy? You killed your brother because you were jealous?'

Shade crouched down, ramming the barrel of the gun into Steve's abdomen. 'Give me some credit, Mr. Allen. Two years ago that rat brother of mine began buying up English Steel shares whenever they came on market. And then just three months ago he convinced that fat, simpleton of a brother, Henry, to sell him all his shares. Do you get it now? Do you understand? The bastard was going to vote me off of my own board. After everything I sacrificed, the self-entitled little shit thought he could take it all from me! They even thought they could compound the insult by beating me at the Helicopter championships.'

'So you decided to kill them? To kill your own brothers?'

Carl laughed. 'Me kill them? Mr. Allen, I am not a killer. I'm a manger. I delegate.' He gestured toward the doorway and Steve turned at the unmistakable sound of high heels on a concrete floor. Dressed once again in black, and looking every bit as alluring as the first day Steve had met her, was Marnie Johnson.

'Hello, Steve,' she said.

Steve looked her up and down, trying to fight the sense of betrayal that blossomed in his chest. 'So you're Carl's attack dog, are you?' he said. 'I have to say, I was expecting somebody taller.'

Marnie didn't answer, instead she pirouetted with baffling speed and sent a devastating side kick into Steve's face. Steve was flung back in his chair, spitting blood and seeing stars.

'Point taken,' he said, blinking as he tried to focus.

Marnie leaned over and dabbed a finger at Steve's cut lip, she looked a while at the blood and then slowly licked it up. 'A girl's got to have a talent,' she said. 'Mine just happens to be killing.'

Steve narrowed his eyes. 'Like you killed your own father?'

Marnie merely shrugged, not the reaction Steve was looking for. 'The man was weak. Useless. His answer to the Skyforce competition was to drink more brandy. We needed a heavy cash injection to carry on at Helispech. So I solved both problems with one rope. I got rid of a weak link, and the insurance company paid me half a million pounds. Pretty good deal, don't you think?'

'I think you're damaged goods, lady.' Said Steve.

Marnie nodded. 'Some guys just can't handle a strong woman,' she said.

Carl looked at his watch. 'As much as I'm enjoying this, we really must start wrapping things up. I've got a schedule to keep, you know.'

Steve ignored him, turning his attention back to Marnie. 'Well if you're so fucking good, then how come you failed to kill me and Martyn the first time, when you sabotaged the pilot's oxygen mask?'

'That wasn't me,' said Marnie. 'That was Richard Jone's cock up. When I kill someone, I do it properly. Like when I pushed my mother down that mountain. You should have seen it, Steve. The look on her face was sheer fucking poetry. Once you've killed your own mum, it really is all rather easy from there on in.'

Steve held her gaze, ever aware of the gun trained on him, waiting for a time to strike out.

Marnie continued, lost in a reverie. 'So, you see, Steve- I prefer to do my killing up close. I find it a more gratifying experience that way. You should have seen my father's eyes when I strangled him in his own car. Too drunk to know what was going on until the last minute, until he knew he was going to die by the hands of his baby girl.'

'You know what?' said Steve. 'I think I prefer your sister.'

Marnie snarled, but her retort was cut off by a sudden shout.

'Hello? Anybody there?'

Steve recognised the Scottish accent of Archie, the mechanic, and braced himself. When Shade made the mistake of turning toward the door, Steve stood bolt upright, using the top of his head to butt the underside of Carl's chin. As the elder Shade brother's head snapped back, Steve made a grab for the gun, but was temporarily distracted as Marnie grabbed a fistful of his hair. He grabbed her wrist and twisted his body around, using his momentum to deliver a heavy upper cut to her gut. She fell to the floor winded, and Steve was already turning back, grabbing Carl Shade's gun hand just as he had been about to pull the trigger. Steve pulled the man's wrist back in a vicious twist, and there were two loud cracks. The first was the snapping of bone in Carl Shade's wrist, the second was the Beretta discharging a round straight through Carl Shade's neck.

It did not take long for his life to end. The bullet blew straight through Shade's adam's apple and took most of his throat out before bursting through his jaw bone. Carl slumped to the floor, hands around his neck, strangled quacking noises emanating from his wreck of a throat. Then his eyes rolled in his head as he suffocated in his own blood.

Steve bent down to pick up the pistol, but it was quickly booted away by Marnie. He didn't waste time in chasing after the gun and leaving his back exposed, he swung round and drove his forearm into Marnie's throat, pinning her against a monitor bank. He raised his knee to protect against the expected kick to the crotch, and grabbed at the hand that sought to claw his eyes out.

'What the fuck is going on here?' came the voice of Archie.

'Grab the gun and cover her, Archie, then call the police!' growled Steve. 'She's a murderer!'

Steve heard the click of the Beretta being readied at the same time he saw the savage grin on Marnie's face.

'Aye, but she's always been very nice to me,' said Archie.

'Shit' Said Steve, for the second time that day.

Marie wiggled out of his grip and dove to the side, leaving Steve entirely exposed. He turned around to face the big Scotsman, who was looking down at him with a sly grin on his face. 'So what's your story, Archie?' he said. 'Scheming brothers? Childhood psychosis?'

'Naw,' said Archie, with a big grin. 'I just like getting paid.'

He fired the Beretta.

THE FINAL FLIGHT

The pain was agonising. Several times Steve had regained consciousness, but the brutality of the gunshot wound that had passed clean though his collar bone would send him sharply back into oblivion. The agony of his shattered bone scraping against itself was unbearable, and Steve's shirt was spattered by the vomiting he had been unable to control.

It was the second time in his life that Steve had been shot, and he had time to weakly reflect that it didn't get any easier.

When he finally gained consciousness for more than a few seconds he ascertained he was in a helicopter- the now familiar noise and the feeling of g-force as the chopper banked were testament to that- but he had no idea where or how high they were. He hadn't dared open his eyes for fear of another bullet that would shut them forever.

The radio crackled through the cockpit speaker system. 'All aircraft this is RAF Waddington. Look out for a runaway at approximately five thousand feet heading out over the English channel overhead Great

Yarmouth, not responding to radio.'

'Shit.' Steve recognised Marnie's voice. 'They're onto us.'

'Just chuck him out now,' came the voice of Archie.

'Don't be stupid,' Marnie replied. 'We have to be mid-channel at least. That way his body will never be recovered.'

'What about Mr. Shade back at Helispech?' said Archie.

'Fuck 'im,' said Marnie. 'Another suicide. He's holding the gun isn't he?'

Archie hesitated. 'I may not be the brains of the outfit, hen, but didn't he have a broken wrist?'

'Oh, for fuck's sake, Archie! I can't think of everything. Nobody even knows he's there yet, we'll sort it when we get rid of this snooping bastard.'

'It all seems a bit rushed,' said Archie.

'That's because it is. We'll deal with Carl's body later. I'll organise a massive withdrawal from his bank account, everyone will think he's done a runner and pin his brother's murders on him. As long as we keep our mouths shut we've got nothing to connect us.'

'That's why I always take payment in cash,' Archie said, roaring with laughter.

Steve never moved, only very slowly opened his right eye. From what he could see he was sitting in the rear of the Augusta 109 with Marnie in front at the controls and the big Scotsman to his left.

The helicopter flew on into the night sky, and Steve had to fight the urge to vomit again.

'Are you sure that twat is dead?' said Marnie.

Steve froze as Archie looked him over.

'If he's not then he will be when I chuck him out the

door, won't he?' said Archie, and the two burst out laughing.

I can see why they get on so well, thought Steve. *They're both a couple of total bastards.*

He used his right hand to start searching the seat to see if there as some kind of weapon he could use to stop Archie pushing him out. He found nothing but the recline lever. He risked a glance at the door. There wasn't even a grab handle to try and hang onto. The doors were electronic.

As if to test the point Marnie suddenly leaned over and pressed a red button. 'Do it now!' she shouted.

The door slid open, revealing an inky void. The noise of the rushing air was deafening. Archie leaned away to undo his seatbelt, and Steve seized the opportunity. He pulled the reclining lever for the seat until he was lying back almost flat. When Archie turned back he was momentarily confused. Steve used that moment of confusion to its fullest, grabbing the back of Archie's head and bringing up his knee hard into the big man's face. Archie fell back, dazed and Steve pressed his advantage, quickly leaning over and pressing the red button above the opposite door. As it slid open he wedged his feet under Archie's huge arse and launched him out into the night and the black abyss of the sea. There wasn't even a scream.

'Steady on back there.' Said Marnie. She was so intent on piloting the chopper she hadn't realised that it was the wrong body that had been thrown to its death.

Steve grimaced as a wave of nausea overtook him. His struggle had left him weaker than ever, and shadows at the edge of his vision threatened to overwhelm him. He shook his head to clear it. To pass out now would surely be his death.

He slowly tried to climb along side Marnie, hoping to get the drop on her. It didn't work. Marnie turned and slammed her fist into his face, sending him sprawling against the chopper's back panel. Steve's eyes widened in fear as the crazed woman threw off her seatbelt and tried to climb into the back with him, murder shining in her eyes. The helicopter began to pitch and yawn crazily. Steve booted Marnie in the face and tried to get upright again, but a sudden movement in the helicopter sent both him and Marnie crashing into the back of the pilot's seats. Steve gulped as he felt Marnie's hands close around his throat. All he could see was her snarling face, like something feral and godless, screaming abuse at him relentlessly. Without the full use of his left arm, there'd be no way he could escape from Marnie's vice-like grip. In a flash of inspiration he took the seatbelt from the seat in front of him and wrapped it around Marnie's neck. He pulled as hard as he could.

The two of them remained like that for some seconds, totally silent as they sat face to face, each trying to kill the other before being killed themselves. Their faces turned red, then purple, then a deep black. Marnie's eyes suddenly popped out, her tongue jutting from her mouth obscenely as her windpipe collapsed utterly. She let out a noise like a rattlesnake's hiss. Steve felt the grip on his own throat go slack as the psychotic woman finally died.

He let out a deep ragged gasp for air, but had little time for relief. As the blood rushed away from his head he once again fought against blacking out. He clambered into the front seat and hit the flashing autopilot button. By the time Steve had managed to get into the pilot's seat harness, the chopper was flying itself.

Ignoring the deep pain in his collar and neck, and fighting a rising tide of panic, Steve tried to assess his situation. He briefly thought about sitting on his hands.

A bit late for that now, he thought.

No pilot. No parachute. No chance, All he could do was wait until the helicopter hit something, or ran out of fuel and fell out of the sky with all the grace and beauty of a plummeting fridge-freezer.

Maybe I can pilot this thing myself, he thought. *Yeah, and maybe pigs might fly.*

Then two things happened simultaneously. The cockpit was filled with a brilliant white beam of light, and a voice came over the radio.

'Steve? Steve is that you?'

For a terrifying moment, in Steve's traumatised mind, he thought that Marnie had returned from the dead. Then a more logical conclusion occurred to him. He looked around the cockpit for a radio or microphone. All he could see above the flight computer screen was a button with the words 'Push To Transmit' written on it. he pressed it with his thumb, switching on the automatic microphone.

'Val, is that you?'

'Yes, its me. Are you okay?'

Steve thought about his situation. 'No,' he concluded.

'Look behind you and to your left,' came Val's voice.

Steve couldn't believe his eyes. A police helicopter was flying in formation with the Augusta. Shining a search light into his cockpit. Steve couldn't help but laugh. 'Pigs might fly!' he said.

'Steve, listen closely because we don't have much time. We're heading back toward the coast and we need to get you out of there before that happens. We're going to try to rocket-fire a rescue line into the rear of the Augusta. Do you understand?'

'Yes,' Steve croaked.

'Stay seated in the front and lean forward,' Val ordered.

Steve did as he was told, fighting constantly against the agony the burst from his shoulder and chest with each heartbeat. Above the noise of the Augusta's engines Steve heard and explosion followed by a loud thud. The whole helicopter started to shake as it began to lean into a shallow dive.

'Steve, you have to pull up- you're dragging us down.' Val's voice sounded urgent.

'I can't pull up,' said Steve through gritted teeth. 'The bloody thing's on autopilot!'

There was a pause from the radio, and a faint whine as the helicopter's dive began to steepen.

'Steve? We haven't got time to send someone over to help you. You'll have to get into the harness and jump clear.'

'I don't know if I've mentioned this, Val, *but I've been fucking shot.*'

'You have to do this, Steve, please. We've only got a matter of minutes before we have to cut the line.'

Steve looked behind him to where the door was still open. He doubted he even had the strength left to climb back over. Thinking quickly he pulled the seats reclining lever and, leaning back, reached over to grab the safety harness on the rocket line. He fumbled as he tried to strap it round his body one-handed.

'Hurry, Steve, we're down to two thousand feet!'

'Thanks for that, Val,' Steve mumbled as he continued to struggle with the safety harness. He clicked the belt around his waist. He had only managed to put his good shoulder and one leg into the harness. It would have to do. Holding onto the harness with his good arm, he shuffled on his bottom along the seat to the open door. He put both legs out of the door and peered out into the darkness. He saw the police copter, now level with and dangerously close to the Augusta. He had time to see also, faintly, the chalk white cliff face of a coastline looming dangerously close, illuminated by the beam of a nearby lighthouse.

Steve jumped. For a moment all he could feel was the rushing of air. The the harness jolted around him, crushing against his wounds with enough force to send him straight back into unconsciousness.

He did not see the police copter veer away from the Augusta as the safety line was cut. Had he been conscious, he would have had the perfect view as the Augusta 109 Power flew straight in to the cliffside, exploding into a brilliant ball of fire, and burning Marnie Johnston's remains to ashes.

THE HOSPITAL

The Queen Elizabeth Hospital in Kings Lynn was the largest and most modern of its kind in the east of England. With its own helipad above the casualty and intensive care unit, the police helicopter was able to fly Steve straight in from the edge of the coast.

Steve now sat in the hospital bed, bored beyond belief. He could barely move, with his arm in a cast and his upper body in a sling. He knew he was lucky to be alive, but he wasn't looking forward to the weeks and months of recuperation as his shattered collar bone healed. He drifted in and out of sleep, the hours merging and blending into a seamless blur.

'Lying down on the job, Commander Allen?'

Steve looked up into the face of his Commanding Officer, Niles Bailey. 'Are my twelve hours up already?' He said.

Niles grinned. 'About two day ago as a matter of fact. How are you feeling?'

'Like I fell out of a helicopter,' said Steve. 'What happened with Carl Shade?'

Niles frowned down at him. 'You probably don't

remember talking to the police officer, but between your story and Valerie's statement, we managed to piece together what had been going on.'

'Val was in on it, too?' said Steve, his heart sinking.

'Oh, good lord, no. As a matter of fact the young lady had been doing a bit of snooping on her own. She found out that Richard Jones and Marnie had a bit of a thing going. He'd take Skyforce Helicopters for supposed test flights, but actually use them for commercial runs for Helispech business.'

Steve nodded. 'Clocking the miles back to cover his tracks.'

'Yes. I get the impression he was in it for whatever Marnie was offering him rather than the cash.'

'She could be quite persuasive that way,' Steve said, bitterly.

Niles sat down at the edge of the bed. 'But obviously his whole operation went to shit as soon as Marnie found out he was being investigated. Forensics were able to find out a few things from his autopsy- mainly that he had been strangled a good while before the supposed suicide.'

'Definitely Marnie's style,' Steve said, grimly. 'And what about McConnell?'

Niles shook his head. 'The only loose end I'm afraid. Crisp is tearing his hair out. My guess is that McConnell has most definitely fled the country by now.'

'Well, I suppose if we threw a blanket over whatever shit he was planning, then that's something we can take away from all this.'

Niles grinned. 'Try telling that to Mr. Crisp.' The C.O stood up and began buttoning up his coat.

'Anyway, I'll take my leave now. I understand you've got another visitor waiting.' Niles tipped him a wink and then walked away only to be replaced by Val Johnston.

'Hi,' she said.

'Hello.' Steve couldn't keep the puzzlement from his voice. 'This is unexpected.'

'I'm sorry if I'm disturbing you-'

'Not at all, your a welcome relief from staring at the ceiling. And besides, I still have to thank you for saving my life.'

Val shrugged. 'It didn't take long for the police to find Carl's body. They thought that Marnie had killed him and was trying to flee the country. They took me along to see if I could talk her down.'

Steve nodded, slowly. 'I'm sorry it worked out the way it did.'

Val shook her head. 'I haven't spoken to Marnie since my father's death. I never really thought that she'd had anything to do with his suicide, but something about it always struck me as wrong. Marnie was always a little... intense.'

'Yes, I gathered that.'

'I'm nothing like her, you understand,' said Val. 'People assume because we look so alike that we act alike, but Marnie and I are very different people.'

'And what will you do? Now that Martyn's dead, what happens to Skyforce? What happens to you?'

Val raised an eyebrow. 'I'm not some impressionable young girl, Steve. I knew Martyn would never leave his wife for me. What we had was... convenient, I suppose. And as for job prospects- there's a whole world outside of Skyforce that'd be glad to have me.'

'Are you sad that he's gone?'

Val nodded. 'He was a passionate man. All that animosity toward his brother, it seems such a waste now. Imagine the team they could have made had they worked together.'

Steve did imagine. It made him shudder.

'I'll go now,' said Val. 'You need your rest and the doctor should be along any minute.' She turned to leave.

'Maybe I'll call you,' said Steve. 'Arrange dinner. Give me a chance to thank you properly?'

Val turned and blushed a little, looking at the floors as a finger went to her lip. 'Maybe I'll call you again,' she said.

Steve grinned as he watched her walk away. He may have been lying broken in a hospital bed, but all of a sudden things were looking up.

*

'Wake up, boyo.'

Steve's eyes snapped open. He'd been enjoying the recuperative sleep he'd slipped into almost as soon as Val left. The hospital looked different now, the quality of the light had changed. Was it night already?

Steve tried to open his mouth and realised with horror that he couldn't. Somebody had taped it shut. He looked around wildly, sucking panicky breaths though his nostrils, until his eyes settled on a figure at the foot of his bed. The man had a shaved head and a light beard and his were eyes hidden behind wire-rimmed spectacles. He was dressed in the smart shirt and tie Steve had come to expect from doctors, and even wore a convincing name badge- but there was no mistaking Michael McConnell.

'That's right,' said McConnell. 'Guess who's back in town?'

The big Irishman walked over until he was leaning over Steve's face. 'I was going to do a runner, to be honest, but when I heard my old friend was in the neighbourhood I couldn't resist dropping by and paying a visit. I would have bought you something, but I couldn't find a florist.'

Steve lashed out with his one good hand, the weak blow was intercepted by McConnell with ease, who caught it by the wrist.

'It'd be the work of a moment to snap your neck, fucker,' growled the IRA man. 'But seeing as you murdered my woman, I thought I'd save something special for you.' McConnell held up a syringe filled with a blue liquid. 'A little concoction of my own. It's mostly lye, though, nothing special. Stick with the classics, that's what I always say. Do you know what lye is?'

Steve nodded his head.

'Good,' McConnell continued. 'Then you'll know what it does to human flesh. I'm going to inject this into your neck, then I'm going to watch as your body dissolves from the inside out. How's that grab you, soldier-boy?'

Steve's eyes grew wide as he saw the needle point approach him. He struggled to no avail with his one good arm.

'I'm going to enjoy this,' hissed McConnell.

In a last lurch of desperation, Steve flung his still

mending arm and cracked McConnell in the head with his cast, letting out a muffled roar as his collar bone broke once again. McConnell stumbled back and Steve launched his body with all his might, snapping the support from the sling and sending him crashing down on top of his assailant.

McConnell quickly scrambled to his feet, his hand clutched over his face, moaning and shaking like a man in a fever dream. Steve was horrified to see that the syringe had embedded itself into McConnell's eyeball. With twitching hands, the big Irishman withdrew the syringe from his eye and flung it aside. He stared down as Steve with mismatched eyes- one now a dark blue where the white should have been.

'I'll see you in hell, solider-boy.' He said. And without a further word he turned and threw himself through the plate glass of the hospital window, a mighty crash disrupting the relative quiet of the hospital.

Steve got slowly to his feet and ripped the tape from his mouth. He shivered and flinched as his body tried to deal with the fresh pain. He felt that he might pass out again- but not before he saw the corpse of Michael McConnell. With grim resolve he lurched over to the window, unmindful of the shocked nurses running into the room behind him. He looked the two floors down at the sprawled figure, seeing the huge splash of dark crimson staining the concrete where the IRA man had landed head first.

Steve shuddered. McConnell had chosen a death on his own terms, escaping the searing agony of the lye eating through his face and into his brain.

'Not if I see you first, boyo,' said Steve, and then

collapsed onto the hospital floor.

EPILOGUE

The Royal teenager loved this time of day. The evening meal was over, his personal bodyguard was next door, phoning his fiancee as he did every evening, and at last he was finally alone.

He could have ripped the parcel open that morning- as soon as he had seen the Civil Aviation Authority postmark- but he wanted to savour it. He opened the parcel and there it was- his helicopter pilot's license.

Once again he felt a deep sense of achievement , the same feeling he had had on the that day three weeks ago when his flying instructor had had told him that he had passed his general flight test. Flying was important to him. Something that was truly his. A way he could escape from the pressures of his life- his school, the media, and yes, even from his family.

Tomorrow was going to be special.

His father had returned from a diplomatic trip to India, and he and his brother were to spend the whole day with him. They were usually forbidden to travel in the same aircraft together, but an exception was to be made tomorrow, when, for the first and last time, the young Royal would prove first-hand his flying skills to his father.

He fell asleep, a look of contentment on his face, still holding the leather bound license in his hand.

It was still dark when his bodyguard drove him speedily away from his uncle's home in Althorpe Hall and they were quickly on to the nearest motorway heading north to the airfield at Bromsfield. He was pleased to find the Skyforce Two plus Two fuelled and ready for him, and after a quick coffee, and after fastidiously performing his pre-flight checks he took off and headed east into the rising sun. He looked over at his new bodyguard.

'Nervous?' he said.

'I've been in a few of these before,' the bigger man replied.

He had arranged to meet his father and brother for lunch at Rambleton Hall, and so had made all the necessary flight plans and received the necessary permissions. Rambleton was, after all, was in RAF Cottesbrooke's Military Air Traffic Zone, and the last thing he wanted was an argument with a Tornado.

Lunch was good, and afterwards, the boy and his father made their way to the helicopter, the bodyguard following behind as usual. The prince wasn't overly concerned when it started to rain as he ran the up the engines to prepare for takeoff. His father sat proudly in the co-pilot's seat whilst his brother sat in the back with the bodyguard.

He bought the helicopter into a fast climb, knowing that the onrushing air would clear the screen of rain. What he hadn't counted on was the body heat of his three passenger. Suddenly, the perspex bubble misted over.

'Damn it,' he said. 'Where's the fan for the demister?' Under pressure the prince selected the wrong control, instead pulling the carburettor heat knob. It made no change to the power of the engine, but it also made no change to the misted-over windows. Becoming disorientated he leaned over and tried to clear the screen with his hand. It had no effect whatsoever.

The words of his instructor were suddenly clear in his head. 'If you lose control you only have sixty seconds to live.'

He looked down at his instruments. *That can't be right*, he thought, *it says I'm in a steep turn, but I'm sure I'm flying level and straight.*

For the first time in his life the prince was truly scared. Beads of perspiration were breaking out onto his forehead, his palms were sweating and his teeth began to grind together. In a sudden moment of inspiration, the answer that should have been obvious from the start finally came to him. He quickly forced open his pilot's door, letting in a rush of outside air. The temperature in the cabin equalised and the screen cleared almost instantly.

The prince's breath caught in his throat as he was able to see in front of him. he was in a steep turn. He quickly pulled the cyclic lever over and applied more power to climb away from the surface of Rutland Water. He let out a long hiss of air through his teeth.

'I thought we might be going for a swim there, son,' came the voice of his father.

The prince looked over and smiled cooly, masking the frenzy of relief he felt inside. Then, filled with the pure joy of flying open skies, he headed southwards to London.

In the back of the helicopter the bodyguard, unaware of the near miss, rubbed at his collarbone- an old wound that was still gave him pain now and then. He sat back to enjoy the flight, looking down at the rolling greens of English countryside beneath him. He was thinking about London, and the woman waiting there for him. He was looking forward to taking a well deserved night off with his wife-to-be.

THE END

ABOUT THE AUTHOR

Bip Wetherell is a former helicopter pilot and helicopter crash survivor. He lives in northamptonshire with his wife Elaine, where he works as a hotelier and musician.

23777098R00116

Printed in Great Britain
by Amazon